Henry Edward Watts, John Parker Anderson

Life of Miguel de Cervantes

Henry Edward Watts, John Parker Anderson

Life of Miguel de Cervantes

ISBN/EAN: 9783337333638

Printed in Europe, USA, Canada, Australia, Japan

Cover: Foto ©Raphael Reischuk / pixelio.de

More available books at **www.hansebooks.com**

LIFE

OF

MIGUEL DE CERVANTES

BY

HENRY EDWARD WATTS.

LONDON:

WALTER SCOTT, 24 WARWICK LANE.

1891.

CONTENTS.

CHAPTER I.

CHAPTER II.

CHAPTER III.

CHAPTER VI.

CHAPTER VII.

6 *CONTENTS.*

CHAPTER XII.

CHAPTER XIII.

PREFATORY NOTE.

———————

THE Life of Cervantes here presented, as one of the series of "Great Writers," is designed to correspond in scale and in character with the literary biographies familiar under that name to the British public. There have been many Lives of Cervantes, of which I have myself written two. The ampler biography prefixed to my edition of *Don Quixote* (1888) was intended especially to serve as an introduction to my translation of Cervantes' great work, in accordance with my theory that the best commentary on the book is the life of the author. It was part of a large scheme which embraced a complete and fully-equipped edition of *Don Quixote*, brought down to the present state of knowledge, on a scale worthy of the book as one of the world's great classics. That edition was so limited in the number of copies printed as scarcely to deserve the name of publication.

The present Life of Cervantes is an entirely new work, built out of the materials which I had collected for my larger edition. It is re-written and re-arranged, with much matter, intended chiefly for Spanish scholars and more advanced Cervantists, omitted, and much else by way of addition in the shape of criticisms and literary history added, to interest a wider circle of readers. For the leading facts of Cervantes' life I have availed myself of all the existing sources of information in Spain and elsewhere, though for the opinions and theories I have adopted I am myself solely responsible.

The translations from the Spanish, except where acknowledged as being by another hand, are my own, the passages from *Don Quixote* being taken from my version as contained in my edition in five volumes of 1888.

H. E. WATTS.

LIFE OF CERVANTES.

CHAPTER I.

"A CERTAIN strong man, of former time, fought
stoutly at Lepanto; worked stoutly as Algerine
slave; stoutly delivered himself from such work-
ing; with stout cheerfulness endured famine and nakedness and the world's ingratitude; and sitting in gaol, with
one arm left him, wrote our joyfullest, and all but our
deepest, modern book, and named it *Don Quixote.*"

This is Thomas Carlyle's brief summary of the life and
work of Miguel de Cervantes. Brief as it is, and true
in all essentials, it is unhappy in combining almost
every kind of popular error regarding a great writer
whose fate it has ever been to be more praised in his
work than studied in his life. Cervantes, though he
bore himself stoutly in captivity, as in every other of the
numerous ills of his luckless life, did not "stoutly
deliver himself," having, after all his heroic attempts at
self-deliverance, to be tamely ransomed. He had not
one arm only, but two arms left him, though the hand
of one was, by wounds received in battle, maimed,

disfigured, and rendered useless. His great book was not
written in a gaol, only begotten there. Lastly, opinion
is divided whether *Don Quixote* is really the "joyfullest"
of modern books. Though designed, in the author's
own words, as "a pastime for melancholy spirits," those
who look for the soul within have found more sadness
than mirth in *Don Quixote.* Certainly, though the
humour is of the deepest, the springs of it lying close
to the fountain of tears, "joyful" is an epithet which
jars upon the sense in connection with the book. It
could have been in no joyous mood that Cervantes, the
old, maimed, and needy soldier, set himself, in the sun-
set of his life, the close of his hopes and aspirations,
to write that burlesque on the chivalric books which is
the dirge of chivalry. For none loved a romance of
chivalry better than he. He had himself drunk deeply
of the draught which had intoxicated his hero. He had
been infected with the same disease as the good Alonso
Quixano. He had shared in the fond illusion that
the function and duty of chivalry was the redressing of
the world's wrongs. He had been a Knight Errant
himself, and his own life the very matter of a romance.
In his youth he had been dazzled with the lustre of a
great enterprise, which seemed to revive the glories of
the heroic age. He had himself assisted at pageants
and deeds of arms which recalled the fabled splendours
and feats of Amadis. Can we conceive him, with his
illusions spent, disappointed with fortune, a man broken
in health and in hope, even though it was at the close of
that long night so fatal to romance and to chivalry, the
reign of the second Philip, entering upon *Don Quixote*
with a joyful heart?—As truly may we speak of *Don*

Quixote as the mournfullest as the joyfullest of books.
May not this be the secret of its extraordinary popularity
and ever-enduring delight that, written to give vent to a
passing humour, which was as much born of a quenched
aspiration and a frustrate longing for the chivalric age
as of contempt and disgust for the vicious and foolish
books of chivalry, *Don Quixote* owes its immortality to
its capacity for reflecting the moods and fancies of all its
readers as well as to its wealth and truth of human
nature ?

To understand the book and its purpose we must
know the author. The life of Cervantes is to the full
as romantic as that of his hero, abounding in strange
adventures and beset with troubles and rebuffs, borne
and encountered with a gallant resolution and a gay
good humour, of the very essence of that chivalry which,
by an odd perversion of his purpose, he is charged by a
great English poet with having " laughed away." Certainly no life is recorded of any man of letters so full of
action, so beset with dangers, so chequered by fortune,
so varied, picturesque, and adventurous. For the story
of that life we have materials in plenty. Born at the
ancient town of Alcalá de Henares, in the province of
New Castile, the seat of a famous university, founded
by Cardinal Ximenes, Miguel de Cervantes was bap-
tised on the 9th of October 1547. From the name
then given to him, it is plausibly conjectured that the
date of his birth was the Michaelmas day preceding, it
being customary in Spain to christen the infants after
the saint on whose day he was born. The date of
Miguel de Cervantes' baptism is recorded in the register
of the parish church of Santa Maria the Greater. That

he was a native of Alcalá, and a *hidalgo principal* of that town, had been mentioned by Haedo in his *Topography of Algiers*, published in 1612. In several official documents Cervantes had written himself and had been described by others, a native of Alcalá; yet his own countrymen were so incurious or so careless of their greatest writer, that for two hundred years the place of his birth was by them undiscovered. By a singular freak of destiny, which might almost look like poetical justice, the very mystery with which Cervantes deliberately surrounded the birthplace of his hero— *cuyo nombre no quiso acordarse*[1]—with the intent, as he explains at the end of the book, that "all the towns and villages of La Mancha might contend among themselves for the honour of giving him birth, as the Seven Cities contended for Homer,"—overtook himself, for his own place of birth was forgotten; and seven cities actually contended, as one or two still, in the face of all evidence, obstinately contend, for the honour of being the cradle of Miguel de Cervantes—these seven being Madrid, Seville, Toledo, Lucena, Esquivias, Consuegra, and Alcázar de San Juan. The last-named town to this day clings to the belief that it produced the real author of *Don Quixote*, and to the sceptical visitor is proudly shown the parish register in which is recorded that "Miguel, son of Blas Cervantes Saavedra and Catalina Lopez," was born on November 9th, 1558. Opposite to this entry, in a modern hand, are written the words, *Este fué el autor de la historia de Don Quixote.* This, of course, cannot be the true Miguel, as, apart

---

[1] See the opening words of *Don Quixote*, Part I., chap. i.

from all other evidence (including Cervantes' own
repeated declarations), the date would alone settle the
question. If born in November 1558 Cervantes must
have been not quite thirteen years of age when he took
a conspicuous part in the battle of Lepanto. That
there was a second Miguel de Cervantes Saavedra
(probably a far-off cousin), whose obscure and worthless
life (he appears to have been a scapegrace) has become
entangled with that of the older and more famous man,
is certain. The first of native scholars who is entitled
to the credit of clearing up all doubts on this subject (doubts which should never have risen) was Juan
de Iriarte, librarian to Charles III., who discovered
among the royal manuscripts a list of certain captives,
redeemed from Algiers in 1580, among whom is
included "Miguel de Cervantes, of the age of thirty
years (he was really thirty-three), a native of Alcalá
de Henares." The question was finally settled by
the learned Father Sarmiento in his tract, *Noticia
sobre la Verdadera Patria de Cervantes*, written in
1761.

The father of our Miguel de Cervantes was Rodrigo
de Cervantes, also a native of Alcalá, and his mother,
Leonor de Cortinas, a native of the neighbouring village
of Barajas. Both father and mother were of good
hidalgo strain though of humble fortune. They were
married in 1540, and had four children—two sons and
two daughters—of whom Miguel was the youngest.
The elder brother, Rodrigo, was a soldier of some
distinction in the wars of Philip. He served with
Miguel in the Levant, was taken prisoner at the
same time, and shared for a while his captivity in

Algiers. He is mentioned as having earned much credit under the Marqués de Santa Cruz in the expedition against the Azores, and died in Flanders, at a date unknown, before Miguel. The elder sister, Andrea, was twice married, and as a widow lived with her brother till the end of his life. The younger, Luisa, became a Carmelite nun in 1561. The father of Rodrigo de Cervantes was Juan, who seems to have been of higher station than his immediate descendants, for he had filled the office of *corregidor* (paid magistrate) of the city of Osuna, and is mentioned in history as the friend and associate of the Conde de Ureña,[1] a grandee of influence in Philip's court. The family of Cervantes (who bore, as their arms, two stags, in punning allusion to their name) came originally from Galicia, and by the early genealogists (who certainly never thought of honouring the author of *Don Quixote*) were traced from the blood of the Gothic kings of Leon. Their direct progenitor was the famous Nuño Alfonso, the warlike Alcaide or constable of Toledo in the eleventh century, whose son took the surname of *Cervatos* (*i.e.*, " a place for stags ") from the castle and lands so designated, which he inherited from his father. This younger son changed that designation for the more euphonious one of *Cervantes*, being the first who bore the name. From him, if heralds and genealogists do not lie, was derived in the male line Juan de Cervantes, who was a *veinticuatro*, or alderman, of Seville in the reign of Juan II., from whom to Miguel de Cervantes the descent is

---

[1] Conde, the Orientalist, was the first to point out that Benengeli (the supposed original author of *Don Quixote*) means in Arabic, " son of a stag."

direct and undoubted.[1] The family branched into La Mancha early in the fifteenth century; and several members of it held command in the military orders of Santiago and San Juan. In order to distinguish himself from others of the same name (the family being rather numerous, as the name is still not uncommon, both in Spain and in Spanish America), Miguel de Cervantes, upon his return from Algiers, in 1580, assumed the additional surname of Saavedra from one of his ancestors, always signing himself thenceforth *Cervantes* (or oftener *Cerbantes*) *Saavedra.*[2]

Of the youth and early years of Miguel de Cervantes nothing is known, except from the slight and too infrequent references to himself which are to be found in some of his prologues and dedications. One of the earliest glimpses we have of the youthful Miguel is from an interesting passage of autobiography contained in the prologue to the Comedies, printed by Cervantes in September 1615, a few months before his death. In this Cervantes tells of his reminiscences of "the great Lope de Rueda," the founder of the Spanish drama, who went about the country with his *troupe* of strollers, acting the pieces he himself had written, with most rustic and primitive apparatus. Doubtless it was from Lope de Rueda, who is described as "the first who brought Comedy out of her swaddling clothes and gave her habitation and decent attire," that the young

---

[1] See the genealogical tree in the appendix to Navarrete, *Vida de Cervantes*, taken from Mendez de Silva (1648).

[2] The labials *b* and *v* are interchangeable in Spanish, and are identical in sound. Hence the joke of Scaliger, of the bliss of living in a country where *bibo* and *vivo* were the same.

Cervantes derived that impulse to the drama which, to the last, in spite of all rebuffs and failures, he was never able to resist. His early education Cervantes received under a teacher of some celebrity in those days, one Lopez de Hoyos, who wrote verses and dedications (as, indeed, what educated man did not in that age?), and was famous for his learning and urbanity. Lopez de Hoyos kept a school at Madrid, the site of which is still remembered, and thither we must presume the young Miguel to have gone from his native town of Alcalá, some twenty miles distant. There is a tradition, too hastily accepted by Ticknor on the authority of Navarrete (who himself had nothing but a baseless theory to go upon in connection with the novel *La Tia Fingida*, attributed, as I hold wrongly, to Cervantes), that Miguel kept his terms at the University of Salamanca. But this legend may be rejected on the score of many improbabilities. Cervantes' parents were hardly in such circumstances as to be able to afford to send their younger son to Salamanca ; nor is it likely that they should have chosen to send him that distance, having a university scarcely less renowned at their doors. There is no proof that Cervantes went to any university; nor was he likely to do so, not being destined for the Church or any learned profession. For such learning as he acquired—and his scholarship, though not profound or exact, was equal to that of the average of the men who wrote in that age, while his general knowledge was superior—he must have been indebted to Hoyos, and to his own reading, which was vast and multifarious beyond that of any of his contemporaries—especially in the literature of his own country and in the poetry of Italy. Hoyos seems to

have entertained for his pupil a singular affection, and
he may claim, in fact, the credit of being the first not
only to detect the promise of greatness in the youth, but
to give a bent to his genius. Upon the sudden and
greatly lamented death of Isabel of Valois, the third
wife of Philip II., the public grief took the form of
innumerable encomiastic sonnets and elegies. Of these
a considerable number were contributed by the pupils of
Lopez de Hoyos, some half-a-dozen of which were composed by Miguel de Cervantes. These, the first favours
of a muse sedulously wooed but seldom kind, are
extravagantly praised by Lopez de Hoyos himself for
their "elegant style," "rhetorical colours," and "delicate
conceits"; and the youthful poet himself (now in his
twenty-first year) is referred to as his master's "dear
and well-loved pupil." More fortunate than the rest of
Cervantes' early pieces, these poems are still in existence,
preserved in Aribau's single-volume edition of the works
of Cervantes, and also in the sumptuous twelve-volume
edition of Argamasilla, which was edited by Hartzenbusch. These early effusions testify rather to Hoyos'
kindliness as a critic than to Cervantes' faculty as a
poet. To this period also may be referred a pastoral
poem entitled "Filena," of which Cervantes, who had
ever a dutiful feeling for his own offspring, though his
tenderness never ran into self-conceit, makes fond,
though obscure, mention in the *Voyage to Parnassus.*[1]
Other sonnets, ballads, elegies, and pieces of verse are
spoken of by Cervantes among the works of his youth,

[1] See *El Viaje del Parnaso,* chap. iv., p. 108, in Mr. J. Y.
Gibson's edition, to which is appended an excellent translation in
the metre of the original (1883).

all of which have perished. Whatever may have been
their quality, it was sufficient to give their author a
certain character in the world, even at this early period,
as a poet, though perhaps Navarrete, his Spanish biographer, speaks too partially of him as being already
enrolled among "the most celebrated poets of the
nation."

CHAPTER II.

I N the year 1568 there arrived in Madrid the Cardinal
Acquaviva, sent by His Holiness the Pope, ostensibly
to condole with King Philip on the death of his son
Don Carlos, but really to negotiate for the settlement
of certain differences in respect of jurisdiction over the
Milanese. This prelate, who was but a year or two
older than Cervantes himself, had acquired already a
character as a *virtuoso* and a lover of letters. He was
fond of the society of men of talent, and would carry
them about with him in public, discussing "divers curious
questions of politics, science, learning, and literature."[1]
Into the service of the Cardinal Miguel de Cervantes
entered as *camarero*, or gentleman of the chamber—an
office implying, in that age, no menial duties, which a
gentleman of birth and education might hold. A scion
even of the proud Mendozas had held it in the previous
generation in the person of the famous Hurtado de
Mendoza, who rose to be the most powerful man in
the State. That Cervantes was recommended to the
Cardinal by his literary accomplishments there is no
reason to doubt. More questionable is the theory which
has been started by some of his Spanish biographers

---

[1] So Mateo Aleman the author of *Guzman de Alfarache*, who
saw his Excellency at Madrid (*Navarrete*, pp. 285, 286).

that Cervantes was moved to enter the Cardinal's service
through his great affection for the Church. In the train
of Acquaviva Cervantes left Madrid in December 1569,
being now in his twenty-third year, taking the road to
Rome overland through the south of France. At Rome
Cervantes remained but a very few months. The air
was full of rumours of war and the din of military
preparation. A new crusade was being organised against
the Turks. The Pope (Pius V.) had succeeded in in-
fluencing the Christian powers of Spain and Venice to
lay aside their differences and to combine with Rome
in a Holy League against the Sultan, whose naval
armaments and encroachments by sea were making him
a terror to Christendom. The call to arms to a youth
of Cervantes' temperament was irresistible. In 1570
he resigned his place in the Cardinal's chamber to enlist
as a soldier in the regiment of Spanish infantry commanded by Don Miguel de Moncada, which regiment
was at that time stationed at Rome as part of a
contingent which had been lent to the Pope by
King Philip. The *tercio de Moncada* was one of
the most distinguished regiments of that famous
Spanish infantry, then at the height of its glory
and at the top of European soldiership. It enlisted
none but young men of good family, for whom it was a
distinction to serve in the ranks. The regiment of
Moncada, with the rest of the Spanish military contingent, was ordered to Naples in the summer of 1570,
there to be reorganised for the great armada which
was being got ready to be launched at the Turk. At
Naples Cervantes tells us that he "trod the streets for
more than a year." The Holy League took some time

to form, and when formed was but a partial and imper-
fect representation of the Christian States—the Emperor
and the King of France not only refusing to join, but
secretly giving information, if not help, to the enemy.
Only Spain and Venice responded to the appeal of the
Pope, and at sea the two behaved rather as rivals than
as allies. Eventually the treaty was signed on the 20th
of May 1571. The allied fleets assembled in the har-
bour of Messina in August, under the command of Don
John of Austria as generalissimo, who had brought with
him thither the Spanish contingent from Naples. The
infantry were distributed among the ships—Miguel de
Cervantes, with a detachment of his regiment, being
placed on board the *Marquesa*, a private ship of Doria's,
chartered by the Spanish Government. On the 16th of
September Don John put to sea with his whole force,
which numbered more than two hundred galleys, with
twenty-four sailing ships, and 26,000 soldiers on board.
No such formidable armament had ever taken the sea
under the Christian flag.

The battle of Lepanto, which for ever demolished the
naval supremacy of Turkey, without materially lower-
ing the Turkish power by sea, was fought on the 7th
of October 1571. Though, for the forces engaged in it
and for the immediate results, it is to be reckoned as
the greatest of sea-fights up to that date and a very
glorious victory, it had not much decisive effect on the
issue of the war. The quarrels between the Venetians
and the Spaniards, who were each more jealous of the
other than angry with the Turk—the dissensions between the commanders—perhaps the youth and inex-
perience of the generalissimo, who, with all his rare

soldierly qualities, was hardly competent to lead so
vast and discordant an array—finally, the superiority
of the Turkish seamanship, and the excellent strategy
of their admirals, combined to defraud the conquerors
of all but the barren laurels of victory.　Still, it was
a great battle, glorious to all who took part in it.
The *Marquesa*, Cervantes' ship, was in the squadron
under the immediate command of the Venetian *proved-
ditore*, Agostino Barbarigo, which formed the left wing
of the Christian fleet.　On the morning of the 7th
October, Cervantes, though ill and weak through a
fever contracted at Naples, insisted, according to the
testimony of his comrades, in being allowed to take a
part in the fighting, and was stationed, in command of
twelve soldiers, on the quarter-deck by the side of the
long-boat (*esquife*).　The left wing, under Barbarigo,
was completely victorious against the Turkish right, and
the *Marquesa*, by all accounts, took her full share of the
fighting.　Among her immediate opponents was the
galley of the Pasha of Alexandria, bearing the royal
standard of Egypt, which was captured by boarding—
Cervantes being among the first to leap on her deck,
receiving in the fight three gunshot wounds in the
breast and one through the left hand.　Fortunately
there has come down to us a minute account of our
hero's behaviour on this day.　Mateo Santisteban, a
soldier who fought alongside of him on the deck of the
Marquesa, testifies before the king's *alcalde* in 1578—
being summoned to speak in support of a petition for
aid presented by Rodrigo de Cervantes, his father—
that he and his comrades prayed Cervantes, when going
into action, to remain below in the galley's cabin, for he

was weak and ill of a fever—that Cervantes replied that if he did so they would say of him he had not done his duty—that he would rather die fighting for God and his king than keep himself under cover and in safety—that he (Santisteban) saw Cervantes fight like a valiant soldier at his station by the *esquife*, where, with other soldiers, the captain had placed him; which testimony is confirmed by Gabriel de Castañeda, another of his comrades.[1] Cervantes has himself given us an animated picture of the fighting in his poetical letter to Mateo Vasquez. I quote from the spirited version of the poem made by my late friend, Mr. J. Y. Gibson, and have the greater pleasure in doing so as neither the original (only discovered in 1863), nor the translation, is so well known as it deserves to be :—

> " And on that happy day, when dubious Fate
>   Look'd on the foeman's fleet with baleful eye,
>   On ours with smiling glance and fortunate,
> Inspired with mingled dread and courage high,
>   In thickest of the direful fight I stood,
>   My hope still stronger than my panoply.
> I marked the shatter'd host melt like a flood,
>   And thousand spots upon old Neptune's breast
>   Dyed red with heathen and with Christian blood;
> Death, like a fury, running with foul zest
>   Hither and thither, sending crowds in ire
>   To lingering torture, or to speedy rest;
> The cries confused, the horrid din and dire,
>   The mortal writhings of the desperate,
>   Who breath'd their last 'mid water and 'mid fire;
> The deep-drawn sighs, the groanings loud and great
>   That sped from wounded breasts in many a throe,
>   Cursing their bitter and detested fate;

---

[1] See *Navarrete*, p. 317, for the full depositions.

The blood that still was left them ceased to flow,
 What time our trumpets, pealing far and near,
 Proclaimed our glory and their overthrow;
The sounds triumphant, ringing loud and clear,
 Bore through the smitten air, in jubilant flood,
 The Christians' victory, from ear to ear!
At that sweet moment I, unlucky, stood
 With one hand buckled firmly to my blade,
 The other dripping downward streams of blood;
Within my breast a cruel thrust had made
 A deep and gaping wound, and my left hand
 Was bruised and shatter'd, past all human aid."

Lepanto has become an empty name. The great victory which rang all Europe through from side to side is forgotten. The brilliant figure of the young conqueror—"the Man sent from God, whose name was John," as Pope Pius in his ecstasy dubbed him—which sheds a passing gleam of romance even over the dull page of Philip's reign—an apparition which must have cheated for a while the youthful fancy of Miguel de Cervantes to imagine that the age of chivalry had come again—has faded out of the world's knowledge. Of all who took part in that famous battle, who included the flower of the youth of Spain and Italy, and the most illustrious captains of the age—it is the private in Moncada's regiment whose memory survives. It is the fortunes of the *Marquesa* galley we follow throughout the fighting. It is Miguel de Cervantes who is the hero of the battle: *Don Quixote*, which has made Lepanto immortal. Still, it would be a poor compliment to the memory of the great writer were we to forget or lightly estimate that which he esteemed as the chief honour of his life—his share in the victory of Lepanto.

In after-life he cherished his hurts received in that fight as his most precious of blessings. He would rather, he says in his reply to his venomous secret assailant, Avellaneda, bear his losses and his sufferings than be whole and have had no share in the glory of the day. He had lost his left hand for "the greater glory of his right." [1]

The recognition of Cervantes' services in the battle, even though those services were rendered in the capacity of a common soldier, was sufficiently notable when we consider that he was but one out of some twenty thousand, though it took a shape which may move a smile. His pay was raised by six crowns a month. He was visited by Don John himself in the hospital at Messina, whither the sick and wounded were taken, and where he was long detained. The wounds in the breast and in the hand tormented him, as we know from his own words, for two years afterwards. His hand was "still dripping blood" at Tunis, where he was engaged under Don John in the capture of *La Goleta.* The use of this hand, which was "shattered in a thousand places," was never recovered, though the popular notion, which has been kept alive by forged portraits and fraudulent statues, that Cervantes was wholly deprived of his hand by a shot or a surgical operation, is erroneous. His own words are that he lost "*el movimiento de la mano izquierda*"[2]—the movement, or use, of the left hand; not that he lost the hand altogether. Nor could he have served as an infantry soldier for four years after

[1] See Prologue to the second part of *Don Quixote,* in vol. iv. of my edition, p. 6.

[2] See *Viaje del Parnaso,* chap. i.

his wound had he been disabled by the total loss of his hand. On the 29th of April 1572, he was sufficiently recovered to leave the hospital at Messina. He then joined the regiment of Figueroa, as famous as his old regiment of Moncada, and took part in Don John's abortive second naval campaign in the Levant, of which so graphic an account is given in the "Story of the Captive" in the second part of *Don Quixote*. The next year he was engaged in the expedition against Tunis. From the end of 1573 to May 1574 he was in garrison with his regiment in the island of Sardinia ; thence, at the latter date, he was transferred to Lombardy, under the orders of Don John. In August 1575 we find him at Naples, whence, there appearing no further prospect of active service, the League being dissolved, and Don John called away from his designs of empire in Africa by his jealous half-brother, Cervantes got leave of absence to revisit his native country. He was furnished with many certificates of conduct and letters of recommendation, of a character and emphasis which we must regard as extraordinary, seeing that he was still but a private soldier, and they who wrote in his behalf were the most illustrious captains and dignitaries of the age. Don Carlos de Aragon, Duke of Sesa and Viceroy of Sicily, wrote to the king and to the Council, in most flattering terms, in favour of "a soldier as deserving as he was unfortunate, who, by his noble virtue and gentle disposition, had won the esteem of his comrades and chiefs."[1] Don John himself, the

---

[1] See *Navarrete*, p. 314. The Duke de Sesa was he who after-wards became Lope de Vega's great patron, in which character he forgot his old friend and fellow-soldier of Lepanto.

commander-in-chief, gave him letters to the king, in which he was strongly recommended for a company, as "a man of valour, of merit, and of many signal services." Provided with these letters, which proved to be of most woful disservice instead of the expected advantage to the possessor, Cervantes set sail for Spain on board the galley *El Sol*, in company with several other distinguished soldiers, including his brother Rodrigo and one Don Pero Diaz de *Quesada*, ex-governor of the Goletta.[1]

It could have been in no very cheerful mood, however fair his prospects of advancement might have seemed, that Cervantes set out to return home. His six years' arduous service had resulted in no bettering of his fortune. His dreams of military glory must have been rudely disturbed. That era of knightly enterprise which seemed to dawn when Don John, in person and character no ill-embodiment of one of his heroes of romance, entered upon his command in the East, had closed abruptly, leaving the promise of great deeds but half accomplished. The vision of chivalry which broke upon the young soldier's eyes when the great fleet went forth to battle upon that memorable morning in October was dissolved. The Turk was beaten, only to renew the fight next year in greater strength. The victories in Africa had been quickly turned to defeat and disaster. The Christian champion—the "man sent from God"—who had begun the fight so gloriously against the Paynim, alas! had been forced to turn his back to the enemy with the duel only half fought out. So ignoble an ending to a campaign so loftily inspired and

[1] "They affirm that his name was Quejada or Quesada."—*Don Quixote*, Part I., chap. i., in vol. i., p. 33, of my edition.

so gloriously begun, might well damp the enthusiasm of a soldier like Miguel de Cervantes and afflict even his sanguine soul with despair of chivalry.

But a still greater affliction was in store for our disillusioned and wounded hero, to extinguish his hopes and to spoil his life. The galley *El Sol*, when almost in sight of the Spanish coast, was set upon by a squadron of Algerine corsairs under the command of the redoubtable Arnaut Mami, an Albanian renegade, the terror of the narrow seas. After a running fight between *El Sol* and three of the swiftest of the pirate galleys, in which Cervantes is reported by his companions to have borne himself valiantly, the Spaniards were overpowered, and had to yield themselves prisoners.[1] They were divided, according to their supposed value—that is, their ransomyielding capacity—among the captors, Cervantes himself falling to the lot of a corsair captain, one Déli Mami, a renegade Greek, noted even among the renegades for his singular brutality. The letters of Don Juan and other chiefs which were found upon him led his captors to believe that he was a person of extraordinary importance, upon whom, therefore, an excessive ransom might be set. Thus the very favours which were conferred on Cervantes, and the acknowledgments which he received for his services, were, by a peculiar stroke of ill-fortune, turned to his greater injury and were the special cause of his suffering. He was brought to Algiers, loaded with chains, and treated with exceptional harshness, in order that, according to true corsair policy, he might be the more eager, being so considerable a personage, to purchase his freedom.

[1] This fight is supposed to be described by Cervantes in his *Galatea*, book iii.

CHAPTER III.

N O passage in Cervantes' chequered and ill-starred life is so full of melancholy interest as his five years' captivity in Algiers. That dismal record called the *Calamities of Authors* contains many a painful chapter; but to no man of letters did it ever happen to endure a torture so exquisite as that which it was the unhappy lot of the author of *Don Quixote* to bear. Camoens, in his old age, half-blind and crippled, begging his daily bread in the streets of Lisbon, is a sufficiently pathetic figure. But Camoens was at least among his own people, and it was by Portuguese, whom he glorified and tried to exalt, that he was starved and neglected. Cervantes, in whom we recognise so many traits, physical and moral, in common with the poet of the *Lusiads*, was in the prime and flower of manhood, with the bloom of his valiant deeds in soldiership fresh upon him, when he was taken prisoner and left to drag out his life in chains, a slave to the hereditary persecutors of his nation and creed. The mind cannot conceive, for one gifted with the poet's and soldier's temperament, at the threshold of what seemed a career full of promise, a more terrible stroke of fortune than that which now fell on Cervantes. Algiers, that den of pirates which had insolently raised itself in the very face of the most potent of the Christian states and barred the road to the inland sea, was then at the height of its power—a power which, strange to say, no maritime nation dared to contest. The armaments directed against the Turk would have sufficed to beat down the walls of Algiers and extirpate that hornet's nest. But for some reason, which those who interpret the policy of nations have failed to explain, none of the Christian states ventured to assail this outwork of Islam, which was ten times more dangerous to the peace and welfare of Christendom than the Grand Signor at Constantinople. Since the time of Charles V. no Spanish monarch seemed to have thought it worth his while to clear the seas of this brood of rovers, though it was Spain which suffered most by their enterprises. In the time of Cervantes, Algiers was a dependency of Turkey, having been conquered from the Moors by one of the brothers Barbarossa, in 1516. The Viceroy, or Dey, nominated from Constantinople, was usually chosen from among the most select of the cut-throats, and was little more than the corsair commodore—his jurisdiction limited to the strip of *littorale* commanded by the pirate galleys, and his revenue derived entirely from prizes taken at sea. The corsair captains were mostly renegades, the converts from Christianity being invariably found to make the most savage and truculent of Mohammedans. In 1575 the Viceroy of Algiers was Rabadan Pasha, a Sardinian renegade. The total population over whom he ruled did not amount, according to Father Haedo (who is the best and most trustworthy authority on all that relates to the affairs of Algiers), to more than 100,000, of whom the renegades, including individuals of every Christian race, formed one-

third. Of the thirty-five corsair captains who are enumerated by Haedo, twenty-four were renegades or sons of
renegades, ten Turks, and one Jew. ' The captives retaining
the name of Christians were estimated at nearly 25,000,
among whom were persons of the highest quality, chiefly
Spaniards and Italians. These were treated, in ordinary
times, with tolerable leniency. The meaner sort were made
to work for their masters, but those from whom ransoms
were expected, though kept in strict confinement, were
allowed considerable indulgences. If the property of the
Viceroy, they did no menial work. They were suffered the
free exercise of their religion, and even to act comedies and
otherwise recreate themselves.[1] The one unpardonable
offence in the captive was attempting to escape, which
was resented by the owner as an invasion of his pecuniary
rights. A price was set upon every slave according to
the local estimate of his worth and quality, the business
of ransoming being a regular traffic, conducted upon fixed
principles, with recognised agents on either side.

Shortly after Cervantes' arrival in Algiers, Rabadan
Pasha was replaced as Viceroy by Hassan Pasha, a
Venetian renegade, a monster of cruelty, noted even
among the Algerines for his lust of blood and singular
brutality. His character is described by Cervantes himself, through the mouth of the Captive in *Don Quixote:*—
"And though hunger and nakedness might trouble us at
times, and indeed almost always, nothing afflicted us so

---

[1] Cervantes himself is said to have written plays to amuse his
fellow-captives. That one of them, however, which is attributed to
him, *La Virgen de Guadelupe* (printed by the Seville Society of
Bibliophiles), could scarcely have been calculated to recreate even an
Algerine slave. I cannot see any trace in it of Cervantes' hand.

much as to hear and see at every turn the till then unheard-of and unseen cruelties which my master (Hassan Pasha) inflicted upon the Christians. Every day he hanged some one, impaled another, and cut off the ears of a third; and this upon so small a pretext or on none at all, that even the Turks acknowledged that he did so for nothing else than because it was his will to do it, and because by nature he was the homicide of the human race (*homicida de todo el género humano*)."[1]

This tyrant, who was said to keep a house full of nose-less Christians for his private entertainment, was master of Algiers during the whole five years of Cervantes' captivity. Very soon after Cervantes was taken, and while he was still a slave to Déli Mami, he made the first of his many attempts at escape. In company with some of his friends, he tried to reach Oran—then a Spanish possession—by land; but the party was deserted by the Moor whom they had engaged for their guide, and were compelled to return to Algiers. Two or three other attempts were made, as Cervantes himself mentions in his comedy of *Life in Algiers* (*El Trato de Argel*); but in every case, though he displayed extraordinary cunning and craft in planning the enterprise, he was foiled, either by the timidity or the treachery of some one of his comrades—he being always the first to give himself up, when the attempt had miscarried, and take the blame upon his own shoulders.

In the second year of his captivity Cervantes managed to communicate with some of his friends at home regarding his own and his brother's deplorable condition.

---

[1] *Don Quixote*, Part I., chap. xl.

His father, Rodrigo, responded to his appeal by raising
a sum of money for their ransom, which was remitted
to Algiers. The money was rejected by Déli Mami
as insufficient for the redemption of a captive so illustrious as Miguel, but it obtained the release of his
brother Rodrigo. The elder brother being free, a
plan was concocted between the two for the deliverance of Miguel and some of his companions, through
the agency of an armed Spanish ship, which was
to appear off the shore on a certain day. This
plan miscarried, as did every other, though through
no fault of Miguel's, whose conduct throughout
was marked by extraordinary coolness, daring, and
magnanimity. In the garden of a Greek renegade named
Hassan, six miles to the eastward of Algiers, was a
cavern by the sea-shore, where, from time to time, some
forty or fifty escaped captives, chiefly gentlemen of
quality, had taken refuge. They were maintained and
supplied with food by Cervantes, with the aid of a
Navarrese slave called Juan. Here they awaited the
arrival of the promised ship from Spain which was to
carry them away—Cervantes being the last to take
refuge in the cavern. The appointed day arrived. A
frigate, sent from Majorca, came off Hassan's garden
in the night, and succeeded in establishing a com-
munication with the captives. Some Moorish fishermen,
however, having given the alarm, the ship was obliged
to put to sea again. Meanwhile there was a traitor at
work, as usual, among those whom Cervantes was risking
so much to save. A certain renegade called *El Dorador*
(*The Gilder*), who had been enlisted in the scheme,
took fright and revealed it to the Viceroy himself, who

sent a strong party of armed Turks to the cavern. Quick to perceive that his plans had failed, Cervantes came forward to declare before the Viceroy's soldiers that he alone had managed the affair, and that none of his companions were to blame. When brought before the Viceroy, he repeated his declaration, nor could he be induced, even with a rope round his neck and the threat of instant death by torture, to implicate any one in his scheme of flight.

There is something inexplicable in the behaviour of the Viceroy on this and other similar occasions, when confronted with this captive. This minister of cruelty, who was never known to spare any one in his wrath, whose daily pastime was torture and mutilation, who had a fancy, revolting even to the Algerine mind, for hanging offenders with his own hands, seems to have quailed before the intrepid bearing of this one Christian slave. According to the remarkable testimony of Father Haedo, who compiled his history of Algiers from the mouths of those who had been captives during Cervantes' time, Hassan Pasha was wont to say that, "could he preserve himself against this maimed Spaniard, he would hold safe his Christians, his ships, and his city." Cervantes himself records, with a pardonable self-complacency, in *Don Quixote*, that "the only one who held his own with him (Hassan) was a Spanish soldier —a certain Saavedra (*i.e.*, Cervantes himself)—to whom, though he did things which will dwell in the memory of those people for many years, and all for the recovery of his liberty, his master never gave a blow nor bade any one to do so, nor even spoke to him an ill word." How are we to account for the strange, unique, immunity enjoyed by Cervantes? That they took him for a person of higher rank than he was is certain; but that circumstance alone, with the prospect of large ransom, would not account for his being spared the indignities and torments to which the highest captives were subject. Some have supposed that they had hopes of converting their prisoner to Mohammedanism, as so many of his bold and fearless nature had been converted. But nothing in Cervantes' life or conduct in Algiers gives colour to this theory. On the contrary, all the evidence goes to prove that he was distinguished among the captives for his correct behaviour, for his benevolence and kindliness of heart towards the poorer Christian captives, and his efforts to comfort them in affliction and keep them steadfast in the faith. Another theory is that Cervantes had a powerful friend at court in the person of one of the corsair captains, one Morato (Murad), called *Maltra-pillo* (*The Sloven*), a Murcian renegade, who was one of Hassan Pasha's principal favourites. This circumstance clearly does not go far enough to explain the influence which Cervantes exercised during his captivity, not only over the Viceroy, but, as a consequence of that perhaps, over the other Christian captives.

In order to keep his dreaded prisoner more close Hassan Pasha purchased him from his master, Déli Mami, for 500 gold crowns; and henceforth, being upon ransom and a slave of the Viceroy's, he was exempt from menial labour, according to custom, though still forced to wear chains. About this time it was, having been now two years in captivity, that he wrote his poetical epistle to Mateo Vasquez, the King of Spain's secretary, which was discovered some five-and-twenty years ago among the archives of the house of Altamira, and forms one of the most valuable of the documents connected with his biography.   In this poem, which consists of eighty-one tercets in the metre of *The Voyage to Parnassus*, the author begins with an autobiographical sketch, reciting his acts and services by sea and land, concluding with a proposal for a general rising of the Christian slaves in Algiers, to be seconded by an armament from Spain.   The king is entreated to complete the work which was attempted by his illustrious father, Charles V.; to destroy the pirates' den; to take pity on the poor Christians, who, with straining eyes, watch for the Spanish fleet to come and unlock their prison doors. The poet is confident that the benign royal bosom is touched by pity of the poor wretches who pine in chains almost in sight of the sacred invincible shores of their native land.   The land of the infidel was weak, the city ill-fortified, and its defenders divided by blood and race —held together only by a common faith and lust of gain.[1]

The adventure was one which was not by any means desperate; and had Philip II. been inspired by any particle of chivalry, or even by any feeling of national duty, he might have succeeded in winning Algiers. Haedo avers that "had Cervantes' fortune corresponded to his intrepidity, his industry, and his projects, this day Algiers would belong to the Christians."   But there is no evidence that the letter to Mateo Vasquez ever

[1] Mr. J. Y. Gibson has translated the epistle to Mateo Vasquez, which will be found included in the volume containing his version of *The Voyage to Parnassus.*

reached the royal eyes. That "benign bosom" (there is always a suspicion of sarcasm in Cervantes' references to Philip II.) was occupied just then with a safer and more tempting adventure—the seizure of Portugal—the throne of which kingdom had become vacant through the disaster which overwhelmed the madcap Don Sebastian and his army at Alcázarquiver.

Undaunted by the ill-fortune which seemed to dog his steps, Cervantes made several other attempts to escape from his abhorred prison. Shortly after his last failure he sent a secret message to the Governor of Oran, entreating him to meet himself and a party of captives at the frontier. The messenger, with Cervantes' letter on him, was seized and brought before the Viceroy, who ordered the one to be impaled and the other to receive two thousand blows with the stick. Once more Cervantes, to the astonishment of Christians and Moslems, was spared—once more to resume his attempts at deliverance. In September 1578 he found a Spanish renegade, one Abderrahman, formerly the Licentiate Giron of Granada, to conspire with him, together with two Valencian merchants resident in Algiers, in a means of escape. These, at their own cost, were to provide an armed vessel, which was to take off sixty of the principal captives, under the direction of Cervantes. The traitor on this occasion was one Blanco de Paz, an Aragonese and a Dominican monk, said to be an agent of the Holy Inquisition, who had for some reason unknown conceived a bitter hatred for Cervantes. This creature, whose mysterious conduct and wholly inexplicable baseness gave Cervantes a good deal of trouble in Algiers, went before the Viceroy to reveal the plot and

denounce the author. The intrusion of the Holy Inquisition (not for the only time) in Cervantes' affairs is a
curious circumstance, which the Spanish biographers have
passed over with the usual reserve when motives of faith
are in question. The fact that the Holy Office had an
agent in Algiers, with free access to the Viceroy, is in
itself strange. Upon Blanco de Paz's information, Cervantes was once more summoned to appear before Hassan
Pasha, public proclamation being made that any one
harbouring him should be punished with death. Cervantes came forward voluntarily, and, presenting himself
before the Viceroy, was seized and bound hand and foot,
with a rope put round his neck, and threatened with
instant death. Again we are told that, moved by his
fearless demeanour and his "ingenious and witty answers,"
the Viceroy was induced to pardon him, ordering him,
for his only punishment, to be confined in the Moors'
prison, which was in his own palace, and laden with extra
chains and guarded with special rigour. The cheerfulness, constancy, and fortitude with which these severities
and his unvarying ill-fortune were borne by Cervantes
won him, says one of the witnesses of his conduct and
fellow-captives, Luis de Pedrosa, "great fame, praise,
honour, and glory among the Christians." We have the
remarkable testimony, indeed, of Haedo, who wrote his
Topography of Algiers upon the information obtained
from various gentlemen of rank and condition who had been
captives in Algiers, to prove that the case of Cervantes
attracted singular attention among his contemporaries,
for the extraordinary rigours to which he was subject,
his daring attempts at escape, and his influence over
his fellow-captives, which seems to have been without

precedent. Haedo (whose book, though not published
till 1612, was written before *Don Quixote* appeared,
and therefore before his testimony could have been
influenced by Cervantes' celebrity as a writer) says
distinctly that the captivity of Cervantes was "one of the
worst there ever was in Algiers." Protracted through
the causes we have indicated, the over-estimate put by
the Algerines upon the value of their prisoner and the
inability of his family to raise the required ransom, it
was destined to come to an end, for the world's good
fortune. In 1579 the large preparations made by Philip II.
for the conquest of Portugal spread terror throughout
Barbary, it being supposed that his real object was a
descent on Algiers. Accordingly, while the hardships and
sufferings of the poorer captives were increased through
the strenuous efforts of the Algerines to add to the
defences of the port, there was a greater eagerness in
the masters to realise their property in slaves, so that
ransoms began to be reduced. The friends of Cervantes
had never ceased their efforts to procure the sum
demanded for his redemption, though it was out of all
proportion to their means. In March 1578 a petition
was presented to the King's Council by Rodrigo Cervantes,
the elder, reciting his son's services, and praying for
assistance to free him from captivity. The Duke of Sesa
backed up this petition, speaking warmly of Cervantes as
a good soldier, who had fought for his Majesty, whom he
had himself recommended for promotion, and who was
deserving of all favour and consideration. The father,
Rodrigo Cervantes, died in 1579, leaving the burden of
Miguel's liberation to rest upon his mother and the
widowed sister, Andrea. The two women managed

between them to raise a sum of 300 ducats, equivalent to £35 in English money. From various other sources another sum of 300 ducats was got, chiefly by way of loan—(a burden which hung round the neck of Miguel for years after)—and the whole placed in the hands of Father Juan Gil, the Redemptorist Father, and Official Redeemer of Castile—a good and holy man, whom Cervantes, in his gratitude, has made immortal.

Father Gil arrived at Algiers in May 1580 with his 600 ducats in gold. But Hassan Pasha would not abate a jot of his demand for Cervantes, which was 1000 ducats, or double the amount he had himself given for this slave to his old master, Déli Mami. Being on the point of returning to Constantinople, on his recall from his government, Hassan had already placed Cervantes on board of one of his galleys, among his other gear, chained and fettered. At the last moment, when the galley was putting off, Father Gil, through his pious entreaties and efforts among the local merchants and others (among whom we should be glad to include the friendly "Sloven"), was enabled to raise a further sum of 500 crowns (*escudos*) in Spanish gold, with which Hassan was satisfied.[1] Then Cervantes was once more a free man, having completed just five years of captivity.

There took place a further delay before Cervantes could embark for Spain, caused by the obdurate male-volence of Cervantes' old enemy, Blanco de Paz. Baffled in his attempts upon Cervantes' life in Algiers, the Dominican had been spreading certain calumnies in

---

[1] The total sum paid for Cervantes' ransom was a little more than £100 of English money of that time—equivalent at this day to £500.

Spain respecting Cervantes' behaviour in captivity. It was necessary for Cervantes, who believed that he had established a claim upon the king for his services, and who looked for civil or military employment of some kind on his return to Spain, that he should come back to his native country with a fair character. The process which ensued seems to have been regarded at the time as unusual, and to us must appear a little superfluous. However, a formal investigation was held in the presence of Father Juan Gil, with all the forms of a judicial inquiry, into the conduct of Miguel de Cervantes during his captivity. A number of witnesses were summoned, including all the gentlemen of note who had been or still were prisoners in Algiers, and the proceedings terminated with the solemn testimony of the judge, Father Juan Gil; for all which the world cannot be too grateful to the memory of Blanco de Paz, who figured as Cervantes' accuser on the occasion. The report of the process, with the depositions of all the witnesses, has come down to us, and it is from it that we are enabled to obtain a most minute, vivid, and pathetic picture of Cervantes' life in Algiers. Had there survived no other record than this to tell us what kind of man Cervantes was before he became a great writer, this would have been sufficient. The enthusiasm, the alacrity, and the unanimity with which the witnesses, who include the captives of the highest rank and character then in Algiers, gave their testimony in favour of their beloved comrade, are very remarkable and most touching. They speak of him in terms such as might glorify any knight of romance ; of his courage in danger, his resolution under suffering, his patience in trouble, his daring and fertility of resource in action. Miguel de Cervantes, during his five years' slavery, had clearly won the hearts of his fellow-captives as completely as he had quelled the fury of his barbarous tyrants and softened their temper.[1]

So ended the fiery ordeal through which the "mutilated of Lepanto" had to pass when yet the world knew him for nothing but a soldier. The story of his life in Algiers, usually passed over hastily by his biographers, it is necessary to tell at large, for it was in that rough school the writer was developed out of the soldier. Algiers, which spoilt his life and ended his dream of romance, roused in him that finer humanity of which *Don Quixote* was the outcome. Throughout all his life and in all his works we see the influence of the hard training which he had gone through in Algiers. How deeply impressed he was by his Algerine experiences, which gave him, doubtless, a larger view of human nature, with a deeper knowledge and a wider tolerance, is made evident in the numerous references he makes to his captivity and to the scenes and characters he had witnessed and studied in that curious little world, with its motley group of people of all races and creeds. Of several of his plays Algiers was made the scene, and his own and his companions' adventures the subject. In several of his novels Algerine corsairs and Christian captives are introduced. In *Don Quixote* we have the episode of the captive Luis de Viedma, doubtless a real passage in the life of one of Cervantes' companions, and the moving story

---

[1] The whole report of the case, with all the depositions of the witnesses, is given in *Navarrete*, pp. 319-349. I have abridged it in an appendix to vol. i. of my edition of *Don Quixote*.

of the Morisco Ricote and his daughter. In all his writings we have the frequent recurrence of Eastern ideas and Eastern expressions, with, what is the most notable fruit of his Algerine experience and a singular evidence of his own good nature and generosity of heart, a degree of tolerance and charity for Mohammedans, which was certainly unusual at that age, and unique in a Spanish great writer.

CHAPTER IV

CERVANTES landed in Spain on one of the last days of 1580. He had been absent just ten years from his native country. He was now thirty-three years of age; and it may be convenient, at this period of his life, to describe what manner of man he was. Unhappily, and to the scandal of Spain, even then entering upon the golden age of her native art, there is no authentic portrait extant of the author of *Don Quixote*. Though said to have been twice painted in his lifetime—by Francisco Pacheco, the master and father-in-law of the great Velasquez, and by Juan de Jauréguy, an artist of eminence—these pictures have been lost or are no longer to be identified. The well-known effigy, in a court suit bedizened with lace and frill, with a ruff of portentous dimensions, all of the period—the hooked nose, big round eyes, and baby mouth—which has stood for the last hundred years and more the counterfeit presentment of Miguel de Cervantes, must be pronounced, for the credit of nature and in the interests of physiognomy, a forgery. A counterfeit indeed it is, but no true presentment. This portrait is a pure fabrication, and a work of fancy, of which the history is not the least of the strange mystifications of which our hero has been the victim. I have told the story in detail else-

where,[1] and need only recapitulate the main facts.
When in the year 1738, the English Minister, Lord
Carteret (who, with other claims to remembrance of
which he has been so strangely deprived, is to be
welcomed as an enthusiastic Cervantist), in order to please
Queen Caroline, published his edition of *Don Quixote*—
the first in any country in which the text was treated
with due honour as a classic, and still, in Tonson's
beautiful type, one of the handsomest—he endeavoured to obtain for his frontispiece a portrait
of the author. But though, as we are told by Dr.
Oldfield in the preface, every effort was made
through the English ambassador in Madrid to find a
portrait of Cervantes, none such could be heard of in
Spain. Therefore, to match the other fanciful illustrations in the four volumes—gorgeous and ghastly sculptures in the Dutch manner by Vanderbank and Vander-
gucht—the English artist, William Kent, was set to
prepare "a representation which should figure the
ingenious author in his great design." William Kent
accordingly "invented and delineated" a portrait of
Cervantes. A three-quarters figure, since familiar to all
the world by his hooked nose and his starched ruff,
supposed to be the ingenious author of *Don Quixote*,
is seated in his library with a pen in his hand, and paper
and ink (for the greater assistance of the imagination) on
a table by his side. His left arm ends in a stump, gaily
frilled. By his side is depicted a knight on horseback
in full armour, with Sancho and his ass in the rear. We
have only to compare this print with all the other

---

[1] In the first volume of my edition of *Don Quixote*, p. 117, etc.

engraved portraits in the Spanish or the English editions, to perceive that they are all copies of this, William Kent's fanciful sketch. That neither the English artist nor the editors of Lord Carteret's *Don Quixote* had any idea of deception is proved by the epigraph in large letters at the foot of the picture : *Retrato de Cervantes de Saavedra por el mismo (Portrait of Cervantes Saavedra by himself)*, meaning, of course, a portrait drawn after Cervantes' own description of his person. On this basis, as I have shown, as the best and most candid of Spanish critics are now agreed, every existing print purporting to be a portrait of Cervantes has been worked. Sometimes the face is turned to the right—sometimes to the left. Generally the lower limbs are omitted, with the stump, the pen, the writing-table, and the other decorative accessories. Everywhere, however, are repeated the hooked nose, the curly moustache, the round eyes, which grow rounder— the baby mouth, which grows smaller—the ruff, which grows stiffer and more newly got up, with every repetition. The editors of the great Spanish edition of 1780, issued by the Academy out of very shame at the homage paid to Cervantes by the foreigner, made a feeble attempt to assert for their own portrait (which was a bust only, in an oval frame) a legitimate paternity. It was taken, they said, from a picture painted by Alonso del Arco, which the Conde de Aguila, a patriotic nobleman of Seville, had purchased from a dealer in Madrid. The first difficulty here is that Alonso del Arco, the deaf and dumb painter, was not born till 1625—nine years after Cervantes' death ; so that his work could have no claim to be painted from the life. Another awkward circumstance, which everybody can detect, is, that the face in the Academy's portrait is identical in feature, in look, and in *pose* with Kent's ideal portrait of 1738. For this mystery the scholars of the Spanish Academy suggested a most ingenious, but, what will appear to all candid minds, a most desperate solution—namely, that it was their own portrait which was the original, and Lord Carteret's the copy—a theory which requires us to believe that the English editors of 1734, having before them a genuine portrait of Cervantes wherewith, for the first time, to adorn an edition of *Don Quixote* and give it value, preferred, out of their preposterous vanity or abundant deceitfulness or sheer perverseness, to make the world believe the real portrait was a sham one.

The facility with which the Spanish Academy in 1780 convinced themselves that their portrait of Cervantes was a true and perfect likeness closely resembles the process by which *Don Quixote* was made to accept the helmet—which in the first essay we learn he demolished with ease—as "a good and perfect helmet," which needed no further trial. Ever since that time the Spaniards have gone on repeating that false image as though it were a real effigy of their Prince of Wits —painters and sculptors reproducing those delusive features, poets singing and patriots gushing over them, until William Kent's ideal Cervantes has become stamped on every one's fancy as the true Miguel. Of late years there has been a revolt against the absurd and childish superstition, led by Spanish critics of the new school of *Cervantistas.* The most enlightened of them reject the Kent portrait and the fable which connects it with a Spanish original. In 1864 the hearts of all true Cervantophiles were rejoiced with the report of the discovery of a new portrait, believed to be the *vera effigies* of the author of *Don Quixote*. The discoverer was Don José Maria Asensio, a gentleman of Seville, who is noted for the enlightened zeal and industry with which he has followed up every trace of Cervantes. The story, as told by Asensio,[1] is briefly as follows :—In 1850, Don José found an anonymous manuscript (not dated), which had once belonged to Don Rafael Monti, of Seville, entitled *Relacion de cosas de Sevilla de* 1590 *á* 1640. In this manuscript it was written that in one of the six pictures, painted by Francisco Pacheco and another for the convent of *La Merced*—a picture representing a Redemptorist Father landing with some captives from Algiers—there was a portrait of Miguel de Cervantes, among other real personages. This statement was confirmed to Don José by a manuscript notice of a collection of portraits in chalk of eminent contemporaries by Pacheco, which (in an incomplete form) is still extant. Induced by these hints to search among the pictures in the *Museo* of Seville (which was formerly the convent *Casa Grande de la Merced*), Don José found one in the series of six described in the catalogue as *San Pedro de Nolasco en uno de los pasos de su vida* (St. Peter of Nola in one of the passages of his life). This represents a boat putting off from shore, in and about which are seven figures, one of which is the saint himself. The others are evidently captives lately redeemed. All are believed, on evidence which has satisfied Señor Asensio, to be portraits of real personages. Among them, conspicuous above all, is a man standing in the stern of

[1] *Nuevos Documentos para ilustrar la vida de Miguel de Cervantes Saavedra.* Seville, 1864.

the boat using a pole, dressed like a sailor, with bare
legs and feet, and a wide-brimmed, low-crowned hat.
His face is turned full to the spectator, as though the
artist wished him expressly to be seen. This, according
to Señor Asensio, is Miguel de Cervantes. There is
much to strengthen and support this conjecture; but
alas! it is only a conjecture. Cervantes might well have
been chosen as one of the captives to be represented in
a scene intended to illustrate the good deeds of the
Redemptorists. His case had made a great noise in
Spain. Moreover, we know that he was a personal
friend and intimate of Pacheco, by whom, we know also,
he was painted. The figure in the boat is a handsome
man in the prime of early manhood, as Cervantes was in
1580. The face, though badly modelled and ill-drawn,
is a singularly fine face, with a broad forehead, beautiful
eyes, a well-defined and rather prominent nose; defective
only in the jaw and chin, of which the weakness has
probably been exaggerated by bad drawing, though it is
true to Cervantes' known defects of character, his in-
decision and infirmity of purpose. Of this portrait
it may be truly said, what cannot be said of its
rival, the hook-nosed impostor, that it might be the
portrait of Cervantes. No lover of Cervantes who
ever looked upon the original at Seville, dimmed
by age as it is and hung in a bad light, but
must have devoutly wished that its claims to be a true
portrait could be verified. Unfortunately they rest only
upon a long chain of conjectures, of which one or two
of the links are rather weak.[1] One piece of evidence,

---

[1] I have a copy in colours of the head and bust of *El Barquero*,
for which I am indebted to the kindness of my friend, Don José

which would have been conclusive, is lacking. The collection of portraits by Pacheco of his contemporaries done in chalks, which has been recently reproduced under the auspices of Señor Asensio, is unfortunately wanting in the sketch of Cervantes. In its absence, we can only hope that something will turn up to confirm our faith in *El Barquero*. Meanwhile we must be content to take Cervantes' own portrait of himself in words, which, in the absence of the promised engraving from Jauréguy's picture, he gave us in the Prologue to the *Novelas Exemplares*, published in 1613:—" He whom you see here, of aquiline features, with chestnut hair, a smooth, unruffled forehead, with sparkling eyes, and a nose arched, though well proportioned—a beard of silver which, not twenty years since, was of gold, great moustaches, a small mouth, the teeth of no account, for he has but six of them, and they are in bad condition, and worse arranged, for they do not hold correspondence one with another; the body between two extremes, neither great nor little ; the complexion bright, rather white than brown, somewhat heavy in the shoulders—this, I say, is the aspect of the author of *Don Quixote* of *La Mancha.*" This description, allowing for the difference of years, tallies exactly with Pacheco's figure of the boatman. The smooth, unruffled forehead, the sparkling eyes, the well-arched nose, are all in the picture. The colour of the boatman's hair is of a ruddy chestnut, and the shoulders—*algo cargadas*— strikingly evident.

Maria Asensio. The engravings of the head in Sir W. Stirling-Maxwell's *Life of Don John* and in the frontispiece of Gibson's translation of the *Viaje del Parnaso*, do not do justice to the picture.

To assist the imagination, in the absence of a pictured likeness, in calling up before the mind's eye the man as he was in his prime of life, let it be added that he was near-sighted, and had an impediment in his speech.[1] From his physical attributes, as well as from the features of his mind and character, we may assume Cervantes to have belonged by blood to the ancient Gothic red-haired and fair-skinned type of Spaniards— the type which seems to be gradually dying out in these latter days, beaten, under the modern conditions of the struggle for life, by the darker, black-haired race— the type to which Camoens also belonged, and the best of the *Conquistadores*, and every prominent hero, fighting and writing man, of the Peninsula from the Cid to Don Enrique the Navigator.

For such a man, on his return to Spain after five years' captivity, the prospect, with Philip the Prudent in full glory, was no pleasant one. Cervantes was now in his thirty-third year, with a spirit unbroken by trouble and a heart which no adversity seemed able to sour. Yet his condition was doleful enough to need all the resources of his gay and sanguine temperament to preserve him from despair. He had come back to Spain, after ten years' absence, blighted in all his hopes, disappointed in the promise of his life, without a profession, without a career, neither a soldier nor a civilian, not knowing whether he was in the king's service or out of it, and with the treasure of the prime talent within him still

---

[1] See *Viaje del Parnaso*, chap. iii.; and the epistle to Mateo Vasquez. Avellaneda, in the bitter, venomous prologue to the false *Don Quixote*, speaks of his rival with incredible brutality as having " more tongue than hands "—*mas lengua que manos.*

undiscovered. To begin the world afresh, as he had to do, he was even less well equipped, except in the matter of experience, than when he was a young man, before Lepanto. His wounds had left him in a great measure disabled for the profession of arms which he had adopted. His chief patron, Don John of Austria, was now dead. Such interest as he had won by his services and good character was already exhausted in the efforts for his release. Those services were precisely, as it happened, those least likely to recommend him for preferment to Philip, who hated the memory, as he had grudged to the victors the glory, of Lepanto. The family of Cervantes was reduced to dire poverty through their exertions to raise his ransom, and henceforward he had to bear the charge of his widowed mother and sister. He himself, without any revenue, was burdened with the debt which had been incurred by his family for his redemption. What was there for the poor maimed soldier of Lepanto to do in the Spain of Philip II.?

CHAPTER V

CERVANTES returned to Spain at the close of 1580, as poor as he had left it ten years before, the richer only in his experience of life and in that liberty which he has declared to be "the greatest gift bestowed by God on man." His hopes of employment in the public service were doomed to be disappointed, so he was driven to resume his profession of soldier, joining his old regiment of Figueroa. That he was enabled to carry a musket in the ranks testifies not only to the fact that his claims to promotion were ignored, but also to his being less crippled by his wounds than is usually supposed. The regiment of Figueroa was now on the frontier of Portugal, forming part of the force under the Duke of Alva which Philip II. was collecting for the invasion of Portugal. It does not appear to have arrived in time to take part in the review of the army by King Philip at Badajoz; nor was there any fighting by land in which it could distinguish itself, the Portuguese resistance being most feeble, and the veteran Alva bearing down all before him by his skill and cruelty combined. An animated picture of life and character in this very regiment of Figueroa during this campaign, is given by Calderon in his play of *El Alcalde de Zalamea*—Don Lope de Figueroa, the well-known commandant, being introduced as one of the personages in the drama. Lope de Vega also, who, it is interesting to know, was himself serving at this date in the ranks of the Figueroa regiment, wrote a play in which this tough old soldier, who seems to have been accepted as the very type of the Castilian man-at-arms, figures as a leading character. The picture which the dramatists give of the internal economy of the regiment is not one which is creditable to the morals or the discipline of the famous *Tercio de Flandés*. The men were badly paid and starved, so that it is no wonder that the habits acquired in the campaign in Flanders, and the severities which it had been accustomed to practise on the heretical subjects of Philip, made it the terror of the country people as much as of the foreign enemy. Cervantes himself in several of his works bears testimony to the lawlessness and recklessness of the Spanish soldier, which were the natural reflection of the stern and barbarous treatment to which he was subject.

Philip claimed the throne of Portugal in right of his mother Isabella, who was sister to King Joam III. But there was another claimant put forth by the native party, in the person of Don Antonio, known in history as the Prior of Ocrato, whose pretensions were supported by France and England. Driven from the country by the superior force and genius of Alva, Don Antonio took refuge with his adherents in the Azores, which he occupied with the Portuguese fleet, strengthened by a contingent of English and French ships. Thither, after a considerable delay, caused by disputes between the military and naval commanders, was despatched, in the summer of 1582, a strong naval armament under the veteran Don Alvaro de Bazan, Marquess of Santa Cruz. The regiment of Figueroa formed part of the expedition, Miguel de Cervantes serving in it as a private, and Rodrigo, his brother, as *alferez*, or ensign—both on board the galleon *San Mateo*. A great battle was fought off Terceira on the 25th of July 1582, in which the Spaniards gained a signal and glorious victory over Don Antonio and his allies—the *San Mateo* bearing, according to the historians, a conspicuous part in the fight, and taking several of the French ships. The fleet returned to Lisbon in the autumn ; but, Don Antonio's partisans again making head, the Marquess of Santa Cruz was a second time obliged to take to the sea in the year following, and Terceira was again the scene of an obstinate naval battle, in which Rodrigo de Cervantes so greatly distinguished himself as to attract the notice of the admiral and secure his promotion. Don Antonio being finally suppressed, the fleet returned to Lisbon, after a series of naval operations, which certainly deserve a place among the most glorious, as they were almost the last, of all the achievements of Spain by sea.

Miguel de Cervantes' own share in these transactions, crippled as he was by the damage he had received at Lepanto, could not have been very great. But in his memorial to the king, presented some years afterwards, he refers to his service under the Marquess of Santa Cruz, and in his sonnets he has celebrated "the great Marquess," that "thunderbolt of war," whose fame in the years following was destined to suffer eclipse.[1]

---

[1] The Marquess of Santa Cruz was the first designated Admiral-in-Chief of the Invincible Armada, but is said not to have approved of the expedition and died a few days after its despatch.

With the return of the Spanish fleet to Lisbon, Cervantes seems to have closed his career as a soldier. He lingered in Portugal for a time, seduced by the courteous and liberal manners of the people, which, as well as the praises of the beauty and grace of their women, he was never weary of reciting. It was in Lisbon that he formed an attachment to a lady, it is said of high birth, of which the fruit was a daughter, Isabel, Cervantes' only child and his constant companion till his death.[1] How deep was the impression left by this romantic episode in his life is proved by the fond and frequent references Cervantes makes to Portugal, and especially to Lisbon, and this in an age when there was even less love between the two races of the Peninsula than there is now. In his very last work, *Persiles and Sigismunda*, written but a few months before his death, he returns to speak of Portugal and the Portuguese with singular enthusiasm, exalting their beauty and high qualities, and commending even their language as sweet and pleasant. Nor was there any attribute of our hero more singular in him than this, his large charity towards all mankind, without distinction of race or creed. He was tolerant even of Moors and of Englishmen, in that fanatical time when the one for their hostility to the faith were not regarded as more outside the pale of humanity than the other for their heresy; nor is there any great Spanish writer of that or any other succeeding age who, steeped as he is in *Españolismo*, is uniformly so courteous to all foreigners.

His military career in Portugal ended, Cervantes seems

---

[1] Doña Isabel de Saavedra, after her father's death, took the veil, entering a convent of barefooted Trinitarian nuns at Madrid.

for a time to have been indulged with hopes of civil employment. At some date, not precisely to be fixed but probably after his return from the second of the expeditions to the Azores, Cervantes was at Mostagan, on the coast of Barbary—then an outpost of Spain— whence he was made the bearer of despatches to the king, by whom he was ordered on a service supposed to be connected with the provisioning of the Spanish garrison at Oran. The service must have been of a trifling and temporary character; and there is no record of Cervantes being employed by the State in any capacity until some years afterwards.

Meanwhile Cervantes must have revisited his old home at Alcalá and formed acquaintances in the district, for out of a new romance which now crossed his life was begotten his first acknowledged work, *Galatea*, a pastoral of mixed prose and poetry, after the Italian model—a model which the Portuguese Jorge Montemayor, in his *Diana*, had recently brought into fashion. A Valencian poet, Gil Polo, had followed Montemayor with his *Diana Enamorada ;* and both pieces were then highly popular and believed to repre- sent the finest culture as imported from Italy. The *Galatea* is written in a flowing, melodious style — a style for correctness superior to that which was natural to the author—profusely interspersed with poems, in the shape of ode, eclogue, and sonnet—abounding in fancy, and what was then regarded as passion. The characters are all shepherds and shepherdesses, but have very little to do, as usual, with sheep. One tells another of a girl who loves him or whom he loves. Sometimes it is the lady who loves the gentleman, and the gentleman will

not. Or it is the other way about, and it is the lady who
is unkind, loving another, who carries on the game by
bestowing his affections on some one else. They all
make long speeches, and have a tendency to break out
into verse, which is as stiff with embroidery as the
shepherdesses themselves. What is to be done with
such themes? The whole life is unreal; the sentiments
false; the passions artificial and affected. No human
genius can make anything of a pastoral; and it is no
discredit in Cervantes to have failed in a kind of composition for which he, of all men, was most unfit. Nor
has any one ridiculed the pastoral life of romance more
happily than Cervantes himself in one of the last
chapters of *Don Quixote;* though it may be doubted
whether *Don Quixote* brought him more fame in his lifetime than *Galatea* had done. Into the body of the
piece is inserted, without any connection with the story,
a long poem called *El Canto de Caliope*, in a more
ambitious strain than Cervantes had yet attempted. It
is so far the most interesting portion of the book as that
it is a catalogue of all the leading poets of Spain, who
are discovered to be very numerous and invested with
the rarest qualities, which nobody but Cervantes (the
most good-natured of critics) has ever been able to
discern. Another feature of interest in *Galatea* is that
most of the characters, perhaps all, are real personages,
disguised under fantastic names. In the shepherdess
Galatea herself is figured the lady whom the poet afterwards took to wife, and for whose delectation the story
is said to have been written. Cervantes himself appears
as the shepherd Elicio; while even so grave and reverent
a personage as Hurtado de Mendoza, the famous

statesman and diplomatist, is represented as a shepherd recently deceased.

Absurd and insipid as *Galatea* is to the modern reader, it is clearly unfair to judge of it by the standards of our time. By his contemporaries Cervantes' pastoral was received with great applause, and we have evidence to show that it brought him immediate fame outside of his country. As a pastoral it certainly compares favourably with other pastorals. Nothing so good in that kind had appeared in Spain. Some of the occasional incidents and episodes are told with all Cervantes' grace and skill as a story-teller. Even to this day the piece may be read (in the original) by young men and maidens with a certain pleasure, and without any harm. The author himself has pronounced, in the famous Inquisition on Don Quixote's library, a very fair verdict on the book which was the first fruit of his genius, by saying, through the mouth of the Priest, that "it contains a little of good invention."

The immediate purpose for which *Galatea* was written was happily accomplished. A few days before its publication, on the 12th of December 1584, Miguel de Cervantes was married at Esquivias, a small town of New Castile, to Doña Catalina de Palacios y Salazar. The young lady appears to have been of a family somewhat superior in worldly circumstances to her husband's; and there is a tradition that one of her kinsmen opposed the match on the ground that Cervantes was not sufficiently endowed with fortune. The tradition goes further, and says that it was in revenge for this opposition that Cervantes made Don Rodrigo de Pacheco, who is identified with Doña Catalina's churlish cousin, the

hero of *Don Quixote*.[1] This legend may be dismissed
with all the other wild theories and speculations which
hang by the silly notion that *Don Quixote* was a satire,
intended for personal application. Not much is known
about Cervantes' wife, who was probably one of the
good wives who leave biographers little to speak about.
She was very much younger than her husband, Cervantes
at the date of his marriage being in his thirty-eighth
year; she bore him no children, and survived him more
than ten years. As in her will she requested to be
buried by his side, we may suppose that she did not
regret her choice. Upon her marriage all her own
goods were settled on her by Cervantes, in a deed which
is still extant, with an inventory of Doña Catalina's
effects, which has a pathetic interest for us as showing
what were the circumstances of the young lady who is
supposed to have brought a fortune to Cervantes. The
list includes several plantations of vines in the district
of Esquivias, and goes minutely into the enumeration
of various articles of domestic furniture—"two linen
sheets, one good blanket, and one worn; tables, chairs,
a brasier, a grater, several sacred images, one cock and
forty-five pullets."[2]

In 1585 Cervantes moved from his wife's town of
Esquivias to Madrid. He now seems to have finally
adopted literature as a profession, despairing of employment in the public service and having no other means
than his pen by which to support his household. In
this were now included his wife, his little natural

[1] See vol. i., pp. 130 and 157, of my edition of *Don Quixote*
(1888).

[2] See Pellicer's *Don Quixote*, vol. i. p. 205.

daughter Isabel, his widowed sister Andrea, with her daughter Constanza, eight years old. All these women were maintained by him for many years—in fact, during their lives and his life, through every phase of his slender fortune.

CHAPTER VI.

M ADRID in 1585 was the centre of a kingdom
which, to all outward seeming, was then at the
height of its greatness and power. The monarch
of Spain, now for the first time ruler of the entire
Peninsula, was lord of a dominion such as till then
never had been on earth. In Europe he held sway,
outside of his own states, over more than half of Italy,
including Lombardy and Naples, with the islands of
Sicily and Sardinia. Tuscany and Genoa were his vassals.
The Duke of Savoy was his dependent. Of the Low
Countries he still held military possession, which the
recent assassination of William of Orange seemed to
render whole and indisputable. By the conquest of
Portugal he had added all her extensive colonial empire
in the East and West to his own. All South and Central
America was his, besides Florida and the Antilles. In
Africa and Asia he possessed vast territories. By land
and sea there was no single power to match that of
Philip II. At home he had contrived to absorb all
right and law into his single person, and was a more
absolute despot than Spain had ever seen. Whatever of
local privileges the states of the Peninsula had enjoyed
under their ancient *fueros* were practically extinguished.
The Cortes met only to register the king's decrees. The

Church, once the representative and champion of the national liberties, had been bribed and coerced in the name of Faith to be the king's right arm and in all civil matters the minister of his will.

In all the arts of luxury and refinement Spain was then the foremost state in Christendom. The wealth of the Indies, then no figure of speech but a very substantial tribute which yearly came to swell the king's coffers, had wrought a great change in the ancient Spanish manners. The sudden and extraordinary influx of the precious metals led to great inequalities of social condition, with a general rise in the cost of living, which tended to increase the national poverty and widen the gulf between rich and poor. The question of whether the discovery and possession of America were productive of any real benefit to Spain—whether they were not indeed the immediate causes of her decadence—has been elsewhere and often amply discussed. The process of national decay had already begun under Philip II., and was doubtless accelerated, if not caused, by the narrow and bigoted spirit with which he dispensed his extraordinary power. The period of Spain's greatest fertility and vigour unhappily coincided with that of her worst corruption and blindest rule. The Church and America together sapped the springs of her growth. All the best manhood of the nation had been flowing now for nearly a century westward, and what America did not receive of energy and intellect was absorbed by the Church. The figures which the native historians give of the enormous multiplication of priests and monks and religious institutions under Philip the Prudent are almost incredible.

5

Never in the history of the world did any state expend so much of its manhood in the service of God. The number of monastic houses within the whole dominion of Philip was reckoned at 60,000; of secular priests over 300,000 ; of monks and friars about 600,000.[1] The Holy Inquisition was then in the very pride and flower of its energy, roasting a heretic about every other day, besides imprisoning and torturing at the rate of some 6000 a year. It sat like an ugly vampire upon the nation, shadowing every process of life, dulling the individual spirit—an abiding terror by day and night. For a genius like that of Cervantes it is impossible to conceive any sphere more hopelessly uncongenial than that which he found at Madrid.

The very fertility of the Spanish mind at this period rendered his prospects, from a worldly point of view, more disheartening. Never was Spain so prolific of writers. The time of quickest growth seemed, by some curious destiny, to have coincided with a season of greatest unkindliness. Though Philip himself did nothing to encourage either letters or art, except so far as they could be brought into the service of the Church —though he is not known to have taken pleasure in any product of human wit—never was the Spanish intellect so busy as during his long reign. In letters and in art there was a spring of life of astonishing force and exuberance. It was the dawn of the golden age of Spanish literature. In poetry especially the outburst was phenomenal. The Castilian tongue, with its double resource of consonant and assonant, lends itself to rhyme

---

[1] See Buckle's *History of Civilisation*, vol. ii. p. 476, where all the authorities are cited.

with a fatal facility. Its very harmonies are a snare to
the true poet. In Cervantes' time, when the language
had attained its highest perfection, almost every one
who wrote was a rhymester who called himself a poet.
Their multitude was so great as to be a standing joke
with the wits. " In every street four thousand poets,"
writes Lope de Vega, himself the most prolific of all.
To write verses was so common an art as to cease to be
a mark of liberal education. Those who could hardly
read, complains Suarez de Figueroa, wrote farces in
rhyme. Cervantes himself, who had but a modest
estimate of his own gift of poetry, ridicules the *poet-
ambre*—the poetastery—" the squadron of seven-month
poets, twenty thousand strong"—"the useless rabble
who attempt to storm the mount when they are not
worthy to stand under its shade."[1]

Amidst this crowd of hungry bards Cervantes had to
struggle for a living, as yet unconscious of his true
powers, and with scanty help from any friend or patron.
He may claim to be the first man of letters who attempted
to live by his pen. Every other great writer of the
period had some preferment, or private source of revenue. Many were ecclesiastics ; others were courtiers ;
all depended on some other means of life than literature.
A public, in the modern sense of the word, there was
none. The patron was a necessary appendage of the
author ; and at this period of his life we do not hear
of Cervantes having any special patrons. For an
original genius of independent spirit the prospect was
gloomy. The publisher, as we know him, did not exist.

---

[1] See *The Voyage to Parnassus*, chap. ii.

There were booksellers, but readers were few and editions
limited.　There was no general law of copyright éven
for Spain.　To make any kind of livelihood by writing,
in such a society as that of Madrid, was about as
desperate an undertaking as the most romantic imagination could conceive.　Madrid had only been made the
capital since 1568, the unhappy choice of Philip II.
Though designated "the only Court"—*La Corte*—it was
far from popular as a residence of the nobility.　Of commerce or of industry there was none.　More than one
city in the provinces excelled Madrid in population, in
wealth, and in splendour and gaiety of life.　To our poet
the struggle for existence must have been a severe one,
though of the details of his life at this period we
know but little.　He had won some fame by his
Galatea, as appears by the flattering allusions to him
in the commendatory sonnets of the time.　He himself tells us that he wrote an infinite number of
ballads—that on "Jealousy" being the one most esteemed
—most of which he supposes are among the damned.[1]
In the ample Spanish *romanceros* and *cancioneros* it may
be that some of these are still extant, if no longer to be
identified.　There are some five or six ballads about the
famous Uchali (Aluch Ali), the Turkish admiral who
brought away the remnant of the Moslem fleet from
Lepanto, which are probably by Cervantes, especially
one, which contains the lament of a Christian slave
for his mistress *Talinca*, which, by reasonable conjecture, is made to be an anagram of *Catalina*,
the name of Cervantes' wife.

---

[1] *Viaje del Parnaso*, chap. ii.

Besides writing ballads and sonnets, it was about this time that Cervantes made his essay as a dramatist, upon a field which, could his genius have fully compassed it, would have been the most profitable of all to him as a writer. The Spanish comedy, which was shortly to develop into such extraordinary grandeur and luxuriance, was then just emerging from its infancy. Lope de Vega had not yet begun to practise his marvellous talent for play-writing. Cervantes, in fact, may be said to be the first of the great writers of Spain who wrote for the stage, his appearance as a playwright being exactly coincident with that of Peele and Marlowe on the English stage. In what year he began to cater for the new taste for the drama, soon to attain, under Lope de Vega and Calderon, to such enormous vogue, and what kind of favour he received, we are not told in any of the histories of the period. Our sole authority for all that we know of Cervantes' career as a dramatic author is an interesting passage in the characteristic prologue to the collection of *Comedies and Interludes*, published by Cervantes thirty years afterwards. He composed, he tells us, about twenty or thirty plays (not included among the number printed), which were all put upon the stage and received with favour—that is, they were acted "without their receiving tribute of cucumbers or of any other missile." "They ran their course without hisses, cries, or disturbances." The names of some of these plays are enumerated by Cervantes in the delightful prose appendix to the *Voyage to Parnassus.* He speaks with special pride of one, *La Confusa* ("The Perplexed Lady"), as "good among the best of the comedies of the Cloak and Sword (*de capa y espada*) which had been up to that time acted." According to Pellicer, he received payment at the full rate, being 800 reals for each play, which was no less than the sum usually paid to the popular favourite, Lope de Vega. Cervantes, in his prologue (full of those touches of modest self-allusion which invest all his prologues and side utterances with so peculiar a charm), speaks of himself as the first who reduced the number of acts in the Spanish comedy from five to three, and also the first who introduced moral and allegorical figures on the stage. Neither claim, as Ticknor has shown, can be maintained; and the second is of more than doubtful merit.

Of all Cervantes' plays only two of those which were represented have come down to us, the *Numancia* and *El Trato de Argel* ("Life in Algiers")—two so different in quality and in style as scarcely to seem the work of one and the same hand. The *Numancia* is a tragedy, having for its subject the siege of the Iberian city so named by the Romans under Scipio Africanus—the most splendid page in the heroic annals of ancient Spain. Cervantes has treated this theme, almost too tragic for representation, with a nobility and passion of sentiment, according to Schlegel and Bouterwek, only to be matched in the masterpieces of Æschylus. In grandeur of conception; in the sublimity of its pathos; in intensity of patriotic feeling and concentrated heroic energy, it would be difficult to find a parallel for the *Numancia* in the whole range of tragedy. Let it be remembered that the drama in Europe was still in its swaddling clothes; that Cervantes was the first in Spain to give shape and consistency to the rude experiments of Lope de Rueda and Naharro. The stage was only just beginning to be evolved from

the booth and the cart of the itinerant showman.
Dramatic art was in its infancy, with no examples but
those of ancient Greece and Rome to direct the modern
playwright. Shakespeare had not begun to write for the
theatre. Corneille and Racine were not born. Italy, to
whom Spain was inclined to look for her models in poetic
art, had as yet produced only the pastoral comedy. The
Numancia must be reckoned as the first play with any
attempt at concerted action and poetical expression which
was put upon the Spanish stage. It was a tragedy such as
no living man had witnessed. That it is deficient in the
ordinary artifices of the stage and sublimely careless of
effect, without a plot in any proper sense, without construction, with nothing to attract the spectator but the
passion and force of national sentiment, and a catastrophe
the most tremendous which any dramatist has ever dared
to introduce into a play—this is what must be said of the
Numancia, which is not to be compared with any other
drama. Cervantes never rose to so high a strain
in poetry before or since. The verse, in spite of its
monotony and its unsuitableness to dramatic action—it
is the *ottava rima* in all the narrative passages—is of
rare quality, with a majesty of thought and depth of
passion such as we may look for in vain in the more
highly developed Spanish drama of an after age. Something of Marlowe's vigour and picturesqueness of expression may be found in the *Numancia*, but Marlowe never
gave us any passages of tender pathos to equal *Liria's*
despairing appeal to *Morandro*—a scene which has moved
even the frigid Ticknor and the judicious Hallam to an
unwonted enthusiasm. The rising of the corpse on the
invocation of the wizard *Marquino* is an effect which, for

sublimity of horror, neither Marlowe nor Shakespeare
ever equalled—without parallel in ancient or modern
tragedy. The wonder is how such a play could ever
have been acted. Yet acted it was, with an effect such
as no play ever reached and with a *mise en scene* unparalleled, on one memorable occasion. When the
French cannon were thundering at the gates and
crumbling walls of Zaragoza, the defenders of the city,
by a happy inspiration, conceived the idea of playing
Numancia before the citizens. The result was to excite
the garrison to such a frenzy of enthusiasm that the
French were driven from the walls and the city
preserved.[1]

August Schlegel is perhaps too extravagant in his
estimate of the positive worth of the *Numancia* as a
drama, and certainly so when he says that it was here
that Cervantes found the true development of his inven-
tive genius. *La Numancia* remains the highest effort of
the author in his serious mood. He never attained
to this height in any other drama. The only other
extant comedy of his, dating from this period, is *El
Trato de Argel*, which is a confused medley of personal
experiences of Algiers, mixed with comedy and sentiment, written in the monotonous octosyllabic verse, with
real characters introduced side by side with demons and
abstractions like *Necessity* and *Opportunity*. It is difficult
to imagine how such a play could have been put on the
stage, and even more difficult to conceive how it could
have been written, even for bread, by one who had, as

---

[1] The *Numancia* has been done into very spirited and flowing
English, with all its various kinds of verse faithfully rendered, by
Mr. J. Y. Gibson.

Cervantes proved afterwards that he had, so true and excellent a notion of the office and character of the drama. Cervantes, however, was not the first great writer who, while perfectly able to make the creatures of his imagination live and move, could not combine them in set scenes to make a play which should be a mirror of life.

Cervantes left off writing for the stage about 1588; he tells us himself, with charming candour, why. He had found other things to occupy him. "I gave up the pen and comedies," he says in the prologue to the *Comedies* printed in 1614, "and there entered presently the monster (or prodigy) of nature (*monstruo de naturaleza*), the great Lope de Vega, and assumed the dramatic throne." It has been disputed whether the phrase applied by Cervantes to his great rival was intended to be complimentary or sarcastic. *Monstruo de naturaleza* may be used in either sense, and perhaps, as Cervantes was fond of double meanings, he deliberately chose the phrase because of its dubiousness. But I cannot help thinking that, seeing the words quoted were written in his old age, when he could no longer be blind to Lope de Vega's bitter and furious enmity, he used them as much in sarcasm as in praise. And considering what had been the relations between the two, and that Lope de Vega (as will be seen hereafter) had more than once attempted to take the bread out of Cervantes' mouth, the reference to Lope's appearance on the dramatic throne is nothing discreditable to Cervantes' magnanimity. Lope de Vega was at this time (1588) twenty-six years of age, being fifteen years younger than his rival. He began to write plays for the stage immediately after his return from the

Invincible Armada, on board of one of the ships of which he had enlisted as a soldier.

Finding himself eclipsed by this new and prodigious comedy-maker, of whom it is reported that he could produce an original play of three acts in forty-eight hours, Cervantes was driven to seek for a livelihood elsewhere and by other means. He does not appear to have finally abandoned the hope of succeeding as a playwright until some years after, for there has been lately discovered the text of a contract, dated in 1592, between him and one Rodrigo Osorio, according to which the latter agrees to give Cervantes fifty ducats each for six comedies, provided they are successful. It does not appear that the payment for the six plays was ever earned; perhaps through failure in the condition annexed.

Before this Cervantes had removed from Madrid to Seville, in quest of the means of life. Seville was then the richest, busiest, and most populous of Spanish cities—the great port for the trade of the Indies—the emporium of the commerce and trade which had been created by the New World. Here Cervantes seems to have been happier and more at home than in the cold and gloomy atmosphere of Philip's capital. That he entered deeply into all the life of this gay and brilliant city, with every phase of which he acquired a profound and minute acquaintance, all his subsequent works bear testimony. *Don Quixote* is full of allusions to Seville—"the support of the poor and the refuge of the outcast," while more than one of the *Novelas* has Seville for its scene. There our author seems to have found friends, through whose interest he obtained a small place as one of four commissaries employed to purchase stores for the fleet in Andalucia. His commission is signed June 12th, 1588. From that date, for some years afterwards, he was engaged in the purchase of oil and grain in the districts around Seville and Granada—an occupation which doubtless furnished him with ample material for his future work, in extending his knowledge of country life and manners. There are still extant, preserved with a care which is in striking contrast with the negligence shown towards all other works of Cervantes, a great number of receipts, invoices, and schedules of expenditure relating to these transactions in grain and oil, all written in Cervantes' clear and bold hand.

In May 1590, sick of the oil and grain buying business, Cervantes made application for a place in the Indies, at that time the universal "refuge and sustenance," as he says, " of desperate men of Spain,"—addressing the king through the President of the Council in a memorial which recited all his services by land and sea, his sufferings in Algiers, his subsequent employment in Portugal and the Azores, " in all which time he had received no preferment," and prayed for one of four offices which he learns to be then vacant—namely, accountant of New Granada, governor of the province of Socomusco in Central America, paymaster of the galleys of Cartagena, or magistrate of the city of La Paz. There is a tradition that this petition was not unfavourably received, and that Cervantes might have succeeded in obtaining one of the places he asked for, had he not been guilty of some indiscretion or negligence not specified. He has himself alluded, in the autobiographical chapter of the *Voyage to*

Parnassus, to certain defects of temperament which
marred his future and spoilt his destiny—defects which,
without any prejudice to his genius or character, might
well have been a bar to his usefulness as an official.

The only formal notice of his memorial was an endorse-
ment by one Nuñez Morquecho, probably a secretary, to
the effect that the applicant "might seek about here (*i.e.,*
nearer home) for the preferment he wants." No such
preferment coming to him, he continued his purchases of
wine, oil, and grain for his Majesty's service. About
this time also he seems to have undertaken the duties of
rate-collector for the State—an office which brought him
an income of 3000 reals, or £30 a year. He proved his
unfitness for this business by over-confidence in those
whom he had to trust, so that more than once he was
brought into money troubles through the failure or dis-
honesty of his agents. The most serious of these was in
connection with one Simon Freire, who was entrusted by
Cervantes with a sum of 7400 reals to carry from Seville
to Madrid. Freire became a bankrupt and fled the
country, and Cervantes had to make good his default.
He was imprisoned for three months at Seville, and
suffered damage to his credit for some years afterwards
on account of this affair, although there was no charge
affecting his personal honour.

During all this period, which is the darkest in his life,
Cervantes did not wholly neglect the pursuit of letters.
It was probably at Seville that he wrote some of his novels,
which were not published, however, until many years
after. In 1595, on the occasion of the canonisation of San
Jacinto, Cervantes entered into the competition for *three
silver spoons* which were offered by a Dominican house

at Zaragoza as the first prize for a poem in praise of the saint, and was successful. In the year after, upon the sacking of Cadiz by the English fleet under Lord Howard of Effingham, Cervantes wrote a satirical sonnet which expressed the popular view of the conduct of the Duke of Medina Celi, who marched in with his beplumed soldiers just when the English earl had departed, after doing all the damage he could to the Spanish shipping. Of this incident of the English irruption Cervantes made happy use in one of the most charming of his novels, *La Española Inglesa.*

CHAPTER VII

ON the 13th of September 1598 died Philip II., after a reign of forty-two years, which must be reckoned as at once the climax and the turning-point of the fortunes of Spain. This is not the place to discuss the character of a monarch who filled so large a space in the eyes of the world. By the majority of his countrymen he is regarded as the model of a judicious and patriotic ruler. He was a true reflex of that Spanish character which he helped so largely to mould, and this, which was the secret of his power, is his best apology. Outside of Spain mankind are agreed to judge him as a cruel, mean, cold-blooded bigot, fitter to rule a monastery than a kingdom, and only wanting courage and energy to be a tyrant. Such a character, the very antithesis of his own, and such an influence, fatal to all true romantic dreams of knightly enterprise which he had cherished in his bosom, could hardly be agreeable to Cervantes, who must have regarded the close of Philip's reign, as we know from many palpable signs the nation did, as the awakening from a long and dark night. I do not mean to support the theory, as started in Spain and elsewhere, that Cervantes was actuated in his works by any ambition to shine as a political or social reformer. He was essentially a man of letters, who troubled himself little about politics, and still less about religion. He was content to take the world as he found it, and was oppressed by no sense of a "mission." He had a good deal of the temper of our own Shakespeare, who, as Ben Jonson reports, was "honest, and of an open and free nature," and did not meddle with the world's bettering, except as it came in the way of his calling. He was too good a Spaniard to be other than orthodox, which is not to imply that he approved of the Holy Inquisition. In that age, and under Philip II., a man had to be careful of what he spoke and wrote. It is only by chance expressions, by side hints, and words of dubious sense, that Cervantes, a master of irony, chose to speak his mind about public affairs on the rare occasions that he did so; yet we cannot be wrong in inferring that he did not approve of the character and system of Philip II. In the first place, in an age when it was the custom in every printed book for the author to pour out a stream of eulogy on the reigning monarch, to laud his wisdom and might, and especially his singular prudence and magnanimity, Cervantes seems deliberately to have avoided doing so. I cannot find any reference to Philip which is without a double meaning, as even the cautious Clemencin is forced to admit.[1] In the *Numancia* he had called the king *segundo sin segundo*— "second without second"—a poor pun, which may be taken either way. In *Don Quixote*, where Charles V. is several times praised with enthusiasm, Philip receives no other notice than once as *nuestro buen rei*—"our good king"—a phrase more contemptuous than respectful.

---

[1] Clemencin's *Don Quixote*, vol. ii. p. 290.

But there is a positive and, as it seems to me, a conclusive proof of Cervantes' feelings towards Philip II. in the sonnet which he wrote on the occasion of the erection of a funeral monument to the dead king at Seville. A catafalque was erected by the cathedral dignitaries in opposition to the civic authorities, and contrary, as it would seem, to the wish of the inhabitants, of a size so monstrous, and decorated so extravagantly, as to excite general ridicule. Cervantes expressed the public feeling in an ironical sonnet, or rather irregular poem of seventeen lines, which he ever afterwards regarded with a peculiar complacency, speaking of it in the *Voyage to Parnassus* as "the principal glory of my writings"—(*honra principal de mis escritos*). Allowing for some humorous exaggeration, these words would imply an extravagant amount of self-laudation could we take them as referring only to the literary merits of the poem. A soldier is speaking, staring at the stupendous erection with startled eyes, vowing that it beggared all description, placing Seville on a level with Rome for wit and wealth. He would wager that to gloat on such a rare sight the soul of the defunct would desert its joys eternal in the skies. It is impossible in any translation to convey the full force of the concentrated sarcasm which almost every word contains, under a mask of simplicity. That the poem won much applause, and was regarded as a kind of event in the life of the city, is proved by the references to it in several of the contemporary chronicles.

It was about this time, when his fortunes seemed to have touched their lowest point—when he was on more than one occasion forced to depend for bread on his

friends, that Cervantes first had that experience of La
Mancha, out of which was begotten the idea of *Don
Quixote*—an idea which, it is important to note, only
took form and shape at the close of Philip II.'s reign.
Between 1599 and 1603 Cervantes was employed in
collecting certain dues on behalf of the Grand Priory of
San Juan, one of the great military orders of Spain,
which held property in La Mancha. Cervantes might
have had some previous knowledge of the district, as
there were members of his family settled in Alcázar,
which is just within the border. In the capacity, never
a popular one, of rate collector, he seems to have given
some offence to the people of Argamasilla, a small town
in the wildest part of that unlovely region. One theory
to account for his unpopularity is, that Cervantes was
concerned in some enterprise connected with the manu-
facture of gunpowder, and that he incurred the wrath of
the people of the neighbourhood by diverting the scanty
stream of their only river, the Guadiana, to the uses of
his industry. Another is, that he had offended a principal
inhabitant of Argamasilla, presumably that same particular cousin of his wife's who had objected to her
marriage, by writing satirical verses at his expense.
Another is, that it was a lady of the place (afterwards
disguised as Dulcinea) who had offended him, or whom
he had offended. However this may be, it is certain
that once, when employed about his business, Cervantes
was laid hold of by some leading person of Argamasilla,
and imprisoned in the cellar of a house called and still
known as the *House of Medrano.* It is a miserable den,
half underground, lighted only by a grating looking on
the street, which remains to this day probably in the
6

same state as when Cervantes was there incarcerated.
How long Cervantes was detained here is not known,
but a pathetic letter of his was extant at the beginning of
this century (now lost), written to an uncle, or probably
cousin, Juan Bernabé de Saavedra, at Alcázar de San
Juan, praying for help and relief, and declaring that
"long days and troubled nights are wearing me out in
this cavern."

That this was the injury, apparently wantonly inflicted,
without any right or law, which caused Cervantes to
cherish a grudge against the people of La Mancha is the
universal belief. Certainly the Manchegans are a people
who lend themselves easily to satire. They are among
the rudest and least cultivated of the races of Spain,
bearing strong traces of Morisco blood, and with a
peculiar expression of mingled simplicity and cunning
in their faces, which Cervantes could not fail to note and
make use of. Argamasilla de Alba, which was the town
whose name the author of *Don Quixote* "would not recall,"
has acquired a renown which to its present inhabitants
is a little embarrassing, though they cannot be persuaded
to regard it as unflattering. Although fallen somewhat
from its old dignity—it was obviously, from the width of
the streets, the character of its buildings, and the size of
its parish church, once a place of greater importance
than it is now—Argamasilla cannot greatly differ from
what it was in Cervantes' time. The *Casa de Medrano*
still stands—a solid structure of stone, with the famous
cellar, lately used as a printing office, whence Rivadeneyra
issued his two beautiful editions of *Don Quixote*—now a
shrine at which good Cervantists worship, and the rare
English visitor pays homage. On the outskirts of the

town stand conspicuous the ruins of what was once a solid house, where Don Quixote is affirmed to have lived ; more by token that there is still to be traced a window out of which the housekeeper pitched the books which were condemned by the priest to the fire. In and around Argamasilla it is safer to doubt of Cervantes than of Don Quixote. Of the two it is the creature rather than the creator who is the living and real presence. Are there not windmills everywhere on the horizon to recall the memory of their inventor? For that Don Quixote was the inventor of windmills is the popular belief. As for Miguel de Cervantes, his name is uttered, with a certain distrust and a shaking of the head, as a wag, who made of Don Quixote a joke, and of his respectable story a fiction.

Next in interest to the dungeon in which Cervantes was imprisoned, and to the house said to have been inhabited by Don Quixote, is the parish church, which is one of unusual size and dignity for so small a town as Argamasilla. In the north transept, in one of the side chapels, is a votive offering in the shape of a picture enclosed in a *retablo*, representing the Virgin, with angels about her, looking down from heaven upon a gentleman and lady kneeling in the act of prayer. The gentleman is about fifty years of age,[1] with high check-bones and lanthorn jaws, robust complexion, wandering eyes, and large moustaches. The lady is younger, and not un-comely. Underneath the picture is an inscription, now to be made out with difficulty, setting forth how that Our Lady appeared to this gentleman when given up by

---

[1] *Frisaba la edad de nuestro hidalgo con los cincuenta años.—Don Quixote,* Part I., chap. i.

physicians, on the eve of St. Matthew in the year 1601, and cured him of a great pain he had in his brain, through a chilliness which "curdled it within" (*que se le quajó dentro*). The portrait is of one Rodrigo de Pacheco, who is known to have been the only *hidalgo* resident at Argamasilla at this period. The lady was his niece. The picture was painted to commemorate Rodrigo de Pacheco's recovery from a mental affliction—he having been the owner of the house which corresponds to the description of Don Quixote's, and is pointed out to-day as his. The picture must have been put up in the church about the time when Cervantes is known to have been in La Mancha. Lastly, it was Pacheco, according to the tradition, who, as the leading man in Argamasilla, clapped Cervantes into the cellar of the house known as the *Casa de Medrano*, probably in some more violent access of "chilliness in the brain."

Here is surely a string of evidence which is almost conclusive as to the source whence Cervantes derived the leading figure and perhaps motive of his *Don Quixote*. Rejecting as preposterous the theory that *Don Quixote* was intended to be a satire on some living person of the time; holding it to be impossible that Cervantes, even if he could have taken a personal grievance so much to heart, could have given it such large utterance and noble shape; we may still admit it to be probable that, having conceived the idea of his book as a burlesque on the romances of chivalry, he borrowed some of the external features of his hero from the life and story of Rodrigo de Pacheco, and perhaps may have been tempted to heighten the picture into a resemblance of the original by the memory of his own wrong. The tradition that it was in the cellar under the House of Medrano that Cervantes wrote his book is untenable. He was not there long enough to write it, nor could he have written it in such a place. I have little doubt, however, that it was here where the idea of writing the book was first conceived, to be carried out afterwards, as we shall see. If my theory is correct that it was the picture in the church of Argamasilla which first suggested *Don Quixote*, the book must have been conceived after 1601. There are other reasons, which it is unnecessary here to dwell upon, why it is improbable that *Don Quixote* could have been begun while Philip II. was alive.

In 1601, Philip III., disliking the site of his father's capital, removed the Court to Valladolid, a city by nature far better suited for a metropolis than Madrid. How Cervantes employed his time in the interval, and how long he remained in the execution of his trivial and ignoble duties in Andalucia and La Mancha, we have no means of learning; but in 1602, at the earliest, he must have begun to write *Don Quixote*. In 1603 we hear of him as removing to Valladolid with his family, doubtless with some desperate hope of sharing in the royal bounty. But Philip III., though of some liberal instincts and with a taste for letters, was a poor weak creature, even more completely abandoned to the debasing influences of priestcraft than his father had been, without any of his father's talent or force of character. His favourite minister, "the Atlas who bore the burden of his Monarchy," as Cervantes called him, was the Duke of Lerma,—the lord of his Sovereign's will and dispenser of his power and grace—a man, according to Quevedo (who spoke with greater freedom than any of his contem-

❧ poraries), "alluring and dexterous rather than intelligent; ruled by the interested cunning of his own creatures but imperious with all others; magnificent, ostentatious; choosing his men only by considerations of his own special policy or from personal friendship or family ties." Under such a man it was not likely that any portion of the king's benevolence should light upon Cervantes. The Duke of Lerma openly professed his contempt for all letters and learning; and as for Cervantes' merits as a soldier, they had now become an old and too common story. Disappointed in his hopes of preferment, Cervantes had to maintain himself with his pen, writing letters and memorials for others, and occupying himself in "various agencies and businesses," says Navarrete, while busy upon his *Don Quixote.* His design must have been known to some of his friends, and it appears that the work was circulated in manuscript before he could find a patron or a publisher. In the first edition of the *Picara Justina*, an unsavoury tale by Francisco de Ubeda, the licence to print which was dated August 1604, Don Quixote is mentioned as though he were already famous; and there is a letter from Lope de Vega to his patron the Duke of Sesa, dated August 4th, 1604, in which there is a malignant allusion to Cervantes and to *Don Quixote.*

It was not until the 26th of September 1604 that the privilege to publish *Don Quixote* was obtained. The copyright, for ten years, was sold to Francisco Robles, the king's printer; the sum received by the author is not recorded. The book was printed by Juan de la Cuesta at Madrid, and published in January 1605.

Cervantes was still resident at Valladolid, nor does he appear to have taken any trouble whatever with the printing of his book. This first impression of Madrid, 1605, was very carelessly made, and swarms with blunders of every kind, typographical and otherwise ; though in respect of the press-work it is quite equal to most of the books printed by Cuesta, the chief printer of Madrid. The title-page bears a shield with Cuesta's device of an arm holding out a hooded falcon, with the motto *Post tenebras spero lucem.* This motto has seriously exercised the wits of some ardent Cervantists, it being absurdly supposed to carry a special reference to the character of the book. It is no more than Cuesta's usual motto, and a common form prefixed to all his books—the "light" spoken of meaning, of course, the light which came of the invention of printing.

The story of Cervantes' quest of a patron and its subsequent results is a very curious one, which has been very attractive to painters, but strangely enough has been neglected by the critics. The patron chosen, apparently not without some effort, was the Duke of Béjar, a principal grandee of the Court, himself, according to a contemporary witness, a poet and a valiant soldier. The choice was not a very happy one, unless we are to suppose that Cervantes made it in a spirit of irony. The Duke of Béjar, of all the noblemen of the day, was the one who might be said to have a special claim to be regarded as the patron of those books of chivalries which *Don Quixote* came to destroy. To his own ancestor —his great grandfather—had been dedicated one of the silliest and dullest of the old romances by the worst and most extravagant of the old writers, Feliciano de Silva, the writer especially ridiculed by Cervantes, whose book, *Florisel de Niquea,* is the very book which is parodied in the opening chapter of *Don Quixote*. The Duke of Béjar himself was noted for his uncommon taste for the books of chivalries then in fashion. It is probable that he took *Don Quixote*, in spite of the queer title, to be a romance of chivalry. We can imagine his disgust and the consternation of his household when the true character of the work was discovered. The patronage lent to the poor author was immediately withdrawn, chiefly at the instigation, it is said, of an ecclesiastic, the Duke's confessor. Then, according to the pleasant story first told by Vicente de los Rios, was enacted that scene which has furnished so frequent a subject to the painters. Cervantes, it is said, begged of the Duke to give him a hearing before deciding against his book. He was permitted to read a chapter, which the Duke found so much to his taste that he graciously revoked his decision, and consented to receive the dedication. There is strong reason to believe, with Hartzenbusch, that the dedication itself was tampered with by somebody—most probably the aforesaid confessor, who, keener of nose than his patron, must have scented something not of the common odour in the new book. The language of the dedication, with its affected and artificial phrases of conventional compliment, is most unlike the style of Cervantes, whose dedications have as marked a character of their own as his prologues. What Hartzenbusch supposes, on the strength of the discovery that this dedication of the First Part of *Don Quixote* is almost word for word identical with Herrera's dedication of his Poems to his patron in 1580, is that Cervantes originally wrote a dedication in a different strain, and that the Duke or some one of his house, not being pleased with it, caused it to be altered by a hand better provided with that "precious ornament of elegance and erudition with which the works composed in the houses of the learned are wont to be composed." Cervantes took his revenge in after years upon this meddling ecclesiastic by bringing him into the Second Part of *Don Quixote*, where there is a passage against those of the religious profession who "govern the houses of Princes," written with a heat and bitterness most unusual in one of his generous and tolerant spirit.[1]

The patronage of the Duke of Béjar does not appear to have done much good either to the book or the author; and from the fact that the Second Part was dedicated to another patron, it has been inferred that Cervantes did not retain the Duke's favour, and that his book failed to please.

[1] *Don Quixote*, Part II., chap. xxxi.

CHAPTER VIII

"DON QUIXOTE" was received on its first appearance with a cold welcome from the author's
friends. The critics and the literary coteries
were puzzled by this strange novelty, and could not
make up their minds at first whether it was more
abominable or admirable. Nothing like this book had
ever appeared in the world of letters. Nothing like it
was expected, it is clear, from Miguel de Cervantes, the
old maimed soldier, whose *Galatea* was now dropping
out of fashion. His age—he was now fifty-seven—his
character, his social position, and what was known of his
romantic antecedents, did not promise a book of humour.
The men of learning sneered at the *ingenio lego*—the lay
or unlearned wit—who had started this new mode of
entertainment, in contempt of the rules and in defiance
of those who made them. The very title was derided as
absurd and vulgar. What of good could come out of
La Mancha? Two of the leading spirits of the age,
Góngora and Lope de Vega, did not disguise their
opinion of the new work—an opinion which perhaps
lost some of its effect from its obvious tincture of envy.
Góngora wrote a satirical sonnet upon the advent of the
English ambassador and the Queen's accouchement in

1605, in which Don Quixote, Sancho, and his ass are introduced in ill-natured connection with the author. Lope de Vega was one of the earliest to give vent to his personal malice against Cervantes, with whom he appears to have kept up, till this date at least, a semblance of friendship. Writing to his patron, the Duke of Sesa, even before the book was published, to give him the news of the town, he says—" Of poets I speak not. Many are in the bud for next year; but there is none so bad as Cervantes or so stupid as to praise *Don Quixote.*" There was, it must be admitted, some ground for Lope's dislike of the book; and seeing that he was then at the very top of his popularity—the "Phœnix of the age"—the darling of princes and delight of the people—we can understand the feeling of consternation with which his parasites and creatures—some of whom never ceased to malign and persecute Cervantes after the appearance of *Don Quixote*—must have read some chapters of the book. There was the daring Prologue—that match-less piece of irony—in which Cervantes had actually "chaffed" the great Lope, taking every kind of liberty with his works, laughing at his pedantry, his vanity, his extravagance. There was the forty-eighth chapter, in which the comedies of Lope are so rudely handled by the Canon of Toledo. All this—in an age when no man dared to speak of the great Lope but with bated breath —a familiar of the Holy Office, too, as one of Cervantes' foulest detractors reminded him in after years—must have caused some little commotion in the circles of the cultured and the literary. On the other side, for the honour of Spanish letters be it recorded, were Quevedo, a kindred genius, always a warm friend and admirer of

Cervantes; and Calderon, who, though belonging to a
generation later, seems to have cordially appreciated
Don Quixote, even introducing the author himself, whom
he always treated with respect, as well as the principal
personages of his story, into his plays.[1] The chorus of
detractors was swelled by all those—chiefly persons of
quality—whose taste in romance had been ridiculed.
Here was a man, forsooth, who tilted against Belianis
of Greece, and dared to enter the lists against Felixmarte, not sparing Florambel or Esferamundi! So bold
an innovation as a book, professing to be of entertainment, in which knights and knightly exercises were made
a jest of,—in which peasants, innkeepers, muleteers, and
other vulgar people spoke their own language and
behaved after their own sordid kind,—had never, since
the revival of letters, been made. Lastly, the great
mass of the ecclesiastics, with a few honourable excep-
tions, with the whole body of their patrons, dependents,
and dupes, though they were too dull to perceive and
too dense to feel the shafts aimed at obscurantism,
superstition, and bigotry, had something more than a
suspicion that *Don Quixote* meant mischief, and was a
book to be discouraged.

In spite of the frowns and sneers of the quality however and the ill-concealed disgust of the learned, who
saw themselves and their affectations and extravagances
calmly thrust aside, *Don Quixote*, there is no reason
to doubt, enjoyed from its birth an unbounded and

---

[1] As indeed Lope de Vega did himself, in his *Cautivos en Argel*
(of which whole scenes are cribbed from Cervantes' *El Trato de
Argel*), where Cervantes is introduced, under the name of Saavedra,
in a not very respectful way.

quite unparalleled share of popular favour. By the general public its reception was most hearty and enthusiastic. The theory that the book hung fire, being deemed to be dangerous, so that the author, in the spirit of Bully Bottom, found it necessary to take pains to assure the public and to "name his name," so that they might not fear, is purely the invention of an impudent *farceur*, one Adolfo de Castro, who, in 1848, wrote *El Buscapië* ("The Squib, or Search-foot"), which he alleged to be the work of Cervantes, and was so taken to be by some critics. There was no need for any such device, for *Don Quixote* was, from the beginning, extraordinarily successful, being received, as the proud and happy author himself affirms, with "general applause by the nations." The king's printer, Cuesta, had to issue a second edition, or rather impression, in the same year, and apparently so quickly upon the heels of the first, that bibliographers are puzzled to know which is the real first edition of 1605. In the same year *Don Quixote* was printed twice in Lisbon, and twice in Valencia. Don Pascual de Gayangos, who is the first living authority on Spanish books, inclines to the belief that there were other editions of 1605 which have perished—one almost certainly of Barcelona, the press of which city was then very active ; one probably of Pamplona, and one of Zaragoza, which were the capitals of old kingdoms. The number of copies of *Don Quixote* issued from the press in the first year was probably in excess of the number reached by any book since the invention of printing. Taking each impression to consist of 500 copies, there would have been printed, according to this estimate, more than 4000 copies of the book in the first year—a figure which was certainly never reached before by any book of entertainment, and extraordinarily large for an age when readers were few and books a luxury—when as yet, though the ancient order of Mutual Admirers was probably in being, there was no recognised system of advertising. Writing some seven or eight years afterwards, Cervantes himself calculated that the number of copies of his book then in print were "more than 12,000," which is no extravagant estimate, seeing that the volume had been then reprinted at Madrid, in Brussels, in Antwerp, in Barcelona, in Milan, and perhaps other of the Flemish and Italian cities under the Spanish dominion. Of all these their popularity has been their ruin. The original *Don Quixotes* have been bethumbed out of existence. This story, written for a passing occasion, became the book of humanity — to use the saying of Sainte-Beuve. "Children finger it; young people read it; grown men are versed in it; grey-beards delight in it," says Samson Carrasco in the Second Part of *Don Quixote*. So many fingers were there from the first to spoil the book, that now a copy of any of the 1605 editions, or even of the Brussels edition of 1607, or of the true second edition of Cuesta of 1608 (the first which has a critical value as being the first which was corrected by the author), is now a prize within the reach of only the most fortunate of collectors.

This extraordinary popularity of a work which it is clear the author himself but lightly regarded—an experiment in a novel kind of entertainment for the first time tried in literature—an essay in a path which he must have trodden somewhat hesitatingly and anxiously, considering that in the new venture he risked both fame and fortune—must have come as a pleasant solace for twenty years of neglect and failure. That Cervantes thought but lightly of his chance of success is proved, I think, beyond dispute by his carelessness in regard to the first edition of *Don Quixote*, which was printed without the author's correction and sent into the world full of the most extraordinary defects. What was written in one chapter is forgotten in the next. Sancho Panza loses his ass, and is found riding on it a little further on. His wife is called now Theresa, now Juana, and again Maria. Names are altered capriciously, times and places are confounded, and gaps left in the narrative unfilled— all which blunders, the matter of stern and malignant comment by his enemies, were an occasion of laughter to the author himself. What are we to conclude from this carelessness? Cervantes, it is true, was living at Valladolid while the book was being printed at Madrid. But it was not till three years afterwards that he seems to have taken any interest in giving shape and symmetry to his work. Are we to suppose that he was ignorant of the good thing he had achieved? This theory would be a little unflattering to his intelligence, and indeed is contradicted by all we know of his character. He must have known the value of *Don Quixote* better than any one else. But it is probable that he began to write in a kind of despair, without any particular design. We have his own words, which ought to be enough, to prove that he had no ulterior or profound purpose, such as some of his critics have pretended to find in *Don Quixote*. He has told us that his object was primarily to produce a book of entertainment—

" Yo he dado en Don Quixote pasatiempo
Al pecho melancólico y mohino
En cualquiera sazon, en todo tiempo." [1]

This pastime was to be given by a story which was to
"destroy the authority and influence which the books
of chivalries have in the world over the vulgar." There
is no reason to believe that Cervantes, at the outset, had
any more serious intention.

There has been written, both in Spain and elsewhere, a
vast amount of nonsense as to Cervantes' presumed real
and esoteric motive in *Don Quixote*. I shall discuss
this part of my subject more fully in a subsequent
chapter, when dealing with *Don Quixote* as a whole. At
present I have to do with the *Don Quixote* as published
in 1605, which, though intended for a complete story,
was afterwards continued in a Second Part. In this, the
First Part, the author's purpose is clearly indicated. It
was to cure the false taste in the romances of chivalry by
parodying their style and ridiculing their extravagances.
There is no reason to believe that Cervantes had any
personal objection to romances of chivalry. He himself
loved a romance, as the shepherd in the maritime Bohemia
loved a ballad, "but even too well." He knew all these
false and foolish books by heart, as perhaps no one else
but the good Alonso Quixano ever did. He had tasted
of all their mischief, and if his brain was not turned by
their reading, it was because that brain was a particularly
strong one. Every line of *Don Quixote* proves how pro-

[1] " And I it is in *Quixote* who have given
A pastime for the melancholy soul,
In every age and for all time and season."
                                    —*Viaje del Parnaso*, chap. iv.

found and minute was the writer's acquaintance with the fustian stuff which he ridicules. He cannot help letting us feel, in that famous Inquisition which the Priest and the Barber hold over Don Quixote's books, how strong is his inclination to this kind of literature. Nor is it all books of chivalries, as such, which he condemns. Some are specially exempted from the penalty inflicted through the secular arm of the Housekeeper. *Amadis of Gaul* and *Palmerin of England* are saved from the fire and treasured as good Christian books. There is a good though perhaps a jesting word even for the unromantic *Tirante the White*, where " the knights eat and sleep and die in beds and make their wills before dying." To argue that because he burlesqued them therefore he hated them is to go against the order of nature. The truth is that it was only against bad romances that Cervantes took up his pen. He hated and despised them, not because they were romances, still less because they were of chivalry, but because they brought the romantical way of writing into discredit and reduced chivalry to braggadocio and rodomontade. The zeal which impelled him was simply a zeal for pure literature. The reform of morals or of manners, except in so far as it resulted naturally from the employment of ridicule against the bad taste in books, was no part of his design. We need not go outside of *Don Quixote* to be convinced that this, and no other, was Cervantes' purpose. Has he not, through the mouth of the shrewd Canon of Toledo, laid down himself the lines on which a true romance should be written ? What is *Don Quixote* itself, as the ingenious Salvá suggests, but a romance of chivalry, which has ruined the fortunes of the others by being

7

immensely in advance of them? Cervantes' own last work, as we shall see, was intended to be a romance of chivalry—which is by no means free from the very errors he has ridiculed. Nay, what was Cervantes' own life but a romance of chivalry?

To estimate the nature of the task which Cervantes undertook and to judge of the value of the service he rendered to literature and to humanity, we have to consider what was the character of those pernicious books of chivalries, and the extent of their influence over the minds of the people of Spain in the sixteenth century. Thoroughly to deal with the subject would need a larger space than I can afford. Even the bibliography of the romances, called of chivalry, would fill a volume. Those who desire to be further acquainted with these books and their history, whose very names would have passed into oblivion but for the one book which ruined them and cast them out, are referred to the masterly *Discurso Preliminar* prefixed to his edition of the four books of *Amadis of Gaul*, in the original Spanish, by Don Pascual de Gayangos, a *resumé* and brief epitome of which I have given in the appendix to the first volume of my edition of *Don Quixote*. An essay upon the growth and history of chivalry in Spain would be out of place in a book like this. Let it suffice for our purpose to say that chivalry, as an institution, lingered in the Peninsula at least a hundred years after it had died out of Europe proper. A century after Chaucer wrote his "Sir Thopas," making mock of the forms of knighthood, the knightly calling was in full glory in Spain. The long duel with the Moor, which only closed with the fifteenth century, had trained the whole manhood of the nation to soldiership.

The trade of fighting was sanctified and made romantic by the presence of the Paynim at her very doors, who possessed the double qualification, as enemies, of being at once of hostile religion and of alien blood. All through that fifteenth century the conditions were perfect for producing the Knight-Errant. He had not far to go in quest of adventure. Mahound and Termagaunt lived just over the border. A dark-featured race which, by a happy chance, was not less chivalrous than the Christians—

> Caballeros Granadinos,
> Aunque Moros hijos d'algo—

were to be easily found when wanted. They were on the other side of the hill or the river. Small wonder then was it that out of that fruitful soil which had grown the Cid and the pre-chivalric warriors there sprang up that ranker produce, the Bohemians of the knightly order— the Knights-Errant. Knight-Errantry, which was a caprice in France or in England, in Spain was a calling. No other country afforded such a field for it, and to no other society was it so well suited. No other country in the fifteenth century could show the world such a scene as that gravely enacted before Juan II. and his court, when eighty knights ran a-tilt with each other, incurring serious loss of limb and damage of person, in order that one of them might fulfil a fantastic vow made to his mistress.[1]

Even so late as the reign of Ferdinand and Isabella, the grave and sober Fernando de Pulgar writes complacently of the noblemen whom he knew who had travelled into other countries in search of adventure, "so

[1] The *Paso Honroso*, held at the instance of Suero de Quiñones in 1434, at the bridge of Orbigo, near Leon.

as to gain honour for themselves, and the fame of valiant and hardy knights for the gentlemen," boasting that of the Errant sort were more Spaniards than of any other nation. The adventure generally ran in this form. A gentleman, clad all in steel, goes out into the wood a-horseback, with his squire behind. To him enters another gentleman similarly clad, regarded by the first as ill-favoured, though nothing can be seen of his countenance. The second gentleman is called upon by the first to confess that the lady he adores is inferior in personal charms to the lady of the challenger. He declines, with injurious expressions. Then they both couch their lances, and, wheeling about to fetch a comfortable distance, gallop their steeds at each other. One is overthrown, upon which the victor inserts the point of his sword within the bars of his opponent's helmet, and makes him admit that his lady is less beautiful than the other's lady. Or there is a dishevelled maiden discovered in the middle of a desolate forest, who is bound to a tree, or otherwise discourteously entreated by a miscreant unsound of religion and large of stature. Her the adventurous knight rescues, slaying her oppressor, and is much put to it, through the lady's loveliness, to maintain his constancy to his own mistress. So runs the course of all Knight-Errantry, with a due admixture of dwarfs, giants, dragons, and enchanters.

The literature which was the product of this chivalry partook largely of its spirit and character. The romance of chivalry flourished nowhere so luxuriantly as in Spain. Indeed, *Amadis* and his progeny are as much racy of the soil as *Don Quixote* itself. The attempt to trace their engendure in the Armorican legends has wholly failed.

There is nothing of the French or Breton character in the romances of the school of Amadis (excluding of course the books of Provençal growth, like *Tirant lo Blanch*), unless we accept the Comte de Tressan's argument that they must be French because of their superior tone and taste. There is reason to believe, indeed, that the Breton romances were known in the Peninsula before any of native growth made their appearance. The first germ of Amadis itself may be Breton, for we know that there was some romance bearing that name current in Spain before the middle of the fourteenth century. How much of that is retained in the Castilian romance as it now exists, which was written after the conquest of Granada (1492), it is now impossible to say and useless to inquire. The conclusion which has been reached by the best authorities is that the *Amadis*, in four books—which is the *Amadis* of *Don Quixote*, pronounced by Cervantes to be "unique in its art and the best of all the books which have been composed in that kind," long supposed to be the work of the Portuguese Lobeira—was composed by a Castilian gentleman, Garci Ordoñez de Montalvo. It was first printed, as Señor Gayangos is of opinion, before the close of the fifteenth century. This is a romance of a far different sort from any of the Breton romances, breathing a spirit more sober, more noble, and more chaste. The life to which we are introduced is as unlike the life of the court of Arthur as Lyonesse is to Trapisonda. The hero himself is cast in a more refined and delicate mould than any of the Arthurian heroes. He has sensibility, tenderness, culture, and even virtue. In the story there is a far more elaborate construction ; there is real pathos and grandeur of sentiment, with no lewdness though much freedom of manners. Nor is Cervantes the only one who has praised *Amadis*. Tasso declared it to be "the most beautiful as well as the most profitable story of the kind that can be read." Sir Walter Scott thought it "a well-conducted story." Compared with the romances of the ages succeeding, the prodigious inventions of Gomberville, Calprenéde, and Scudery, it is vastly better — cleaner, more orderly, more interesting, with more of art as well as of nature. The heroes fight too often and win too easily. We are so assured of their triumph over the miscreant Paynim and the discourteous giantry, that the record of their perpetual victories becomes a little tedious. But it is very good fighting, which cannot be said of some later attempts in that kind. The slaughter is conducted in an artistic way, by none of your amateur murder-mongers, but those who knew how men were killed, and wrote for a public well experienced in killing. And, after all, the exploits of Amadis are not more wonderful than those of the British baronet of modern romance.

Of the race of which Amadis was the progenitor—the Lisuartes, Florisandros, Florisels—down to the fourteenth book claiming to be of *Amadis*, with the Palmerins (except that "Palm of England" which the priest saved from the *auto-de-fé*), and the heroes of the "Galo-Grecian" and the Greco-Asiatic cycles, and the heroic books, Provençal, independent, and Christian—nothing need be said but that they are incredibly bad and stupid. Against these it was that Cervantes directed his ridicule in *Don Quixote*. The extent to which the public morals as well as the public taste (for be it understood that the successors of Amadis departed very widely from their ancestor in morals as in manners) were corrupted by this kind of reading, we may estimate from the unanimous testimony of moralists and historians. In vain did the Church and the Cortes fulminate and issue decrees against the pernicious habit. All Spain was given up to the reading of those "romantical books." They formed the model on which society based its life and its talk. Courtiers spoke no other language. Lovers wooed like Amadis, and their mistresses too often loved like Oriana. Even the grave Charles the Fifth, who issued decrees against the books, chose *Belianis of Greece* for his favourite reading. The potent and solid Mendoza took with him, when sent on an embassy to Rome, *Amadis* and *Celestina* for his only library. Ignatius Loyola (whom some have wickedly imagined to be satirised in *Don Quixote*) founded his idea of a Christian order upon that of chivalry. Even the sainted Teresa, glory of Spanish piety, not only was given up to the reading of these vain books but is reputed to have written some herself. For the country people the only entertainment was the reading of these books, which came to be received as gospel truth. What says the innkeeper when the priest tries to persuade him that *Felixmarte of Hyrcania* and *Cirongilio of Thrace* were lying books, full of frenzies and follies? "To another dog with that bone!—as though I knew not how many beans make five or where my shoe pinches me. A good thing indeed that your worship should wish to persuade me that all which these fine books say are but follies and lies—they, printed with the licence of the Lords of the King's Council—as if they were people who would allow such a pack of lies to be printed—and so many battles and enchantments as take away one's wits."[1]   Many of those who took to this reading, both high and low, believed that these heroes once really lived and performed the exploits set down for them.   Was there not a Portuguese poet once swore upon the Evangelists that *Amadis* was all true?   There is a pleasant story, cited by Ticknor from the *Arte de Galanteria*, of a knight who came home one day from the chase, and found his women all in tears.   Asking them why they wept—"Sir," they replied, "Amadis is dead." They had come to the 174th chapter of the eighth book, which is specially devoted to the chronicling of the deeds of Lisuarte of Greece, a nephew of Amadis.

From the single fact that, from first to last, there were produced in Spain over seventy romances of chivalry, most of them longer than a modern novel, we may judge of the enormous hold which this species of literature had taken on the national mind, and also of the arduous nature of the adventure to which Cervantes devoted himself, of rooting up and destroying the whole pernicious brood.   How completely he succeeded, and what excellent knight's service was done by his *Don Quixote*, is proved by the fact that from 1605 not one new book of chivalry was written, nor one old one printed.   Such a revolution in taste was never accomplished by any writer before or since.   The doughtiest knight of romance never achieved an adventure so stupendous.   With his pen, keener than the lance of mythic or imaginary

---

[1] *Don Quixote*, Part I., chap. xxxii.

hero, he slew the whole army of puissant cavaliers, very valiant and accomplished lovers—making havoc of the Primaleons and Polindos, conquering those invincible ones, scattering the puissant and the ever-victorious, and leaving the entire show in as great rout and confusion as Don Quixote left Master Peter's puppets, "with all the fittings hacked to pieces and made mincemeat, the King Marsilio badly wounded, and the Emperor Charlemagne with his crown and head split in two."[1]

[1] *Don Quixote*, Part I., chap. xxvi.

CHAPTER IX

THE success of *Don Quixote* seems to have been of scant profit to the author. Such glimpses as we have of Cervantes' life at Valladolid show him to be still battling against the ill fortune which never ceased to dog his steps, and was now preparing for him fresh humiliations. The direct receipts from his book were doubtless small, and from his allusions to their tricks in the Second Part we may judge that the author was not over pleased with his publishers.

"Prithee tell me, sir," asks Don Quixote of an author in Barcelona, "is this book being printed on your own account, or has the copyright been sold to a bookseller?"

"I print it on my own account," answered the author; "and I expect to gain at least a thousand ducats by this first edition, which is to be of two thousand copies, and they will go off in a trice at six reals a-piece."

"You are mighty good at the reckoning," responded Don Quixote; "it is very clear that you do not know the ins and outs of the publishers, and the understandings they have with one another. I promise you that when you are saddled with two thousand copies of a book you will find your shoulders so sore as to frighten you, and especially if the book is a little out of the common, and nothing piquant."

Doubtless Cervantes was speaking of his own painful experience. In his novel of *The Licentiate Glass-house* he notices one of the devices of the publishing trade, which was to buy the right of printing fifteen hundred copies from the author, and to print and sell three thousand. From the more distant publishers in Lisbon, Barcelona, and Valencia, who reprinted *Don Quixote* on its first appearance, it may be doubted whether Cervantes received any payment at all. In those days to live by writing books alone was what no man had attempted. The pen which had written *Don Quixote* was employed, perhaps more profitably, in writing letters and petitions, and transcribing formal documents—sometimes, it is said, of State, but generally for individuals. Valladolid, as the seat of the Court, was the resort of all the most famous of the men of letters ; and among these Cervantes found friends. That he made others by his book is probable, though we know of the success of *Don Quixote* among the wits of the age rather by the sarcasms of those he had offended than the praises of those he had pleased. Among those who could not forgive Cervantes for writing *Don Quixote* was Luis de Góngora, then giving up that pure and simple style which had made him the first of the living poets of Spain, to plunge into the abyss of Gongorism. A satirical sonnet written by Góngora on the occasion of the coming of the English ambassador, Lord Nottingham, in May 1605, contains one of the earliest references to *Don Quixote*. Apparently Góngora was disgusted with the attentions paid by the Spanish Court to the " Lutheran," and gave vent to what was probably the feeling in the ultra-national and orthodox circles, in lines less conspicuous

by wit than by ill-humour and jealousy. The sonnet
concludes with a reference to Cervantes :—

> " Unto Don Quixote the commandment ran
> To write these deeds—to Sancho and his ass."

The point of the sarcasm is not very clear, but the
shaft is evidently levelled at the character thus early
earned by Cervantes of one who earned fame by ridiculing the national weaknesses. By the mandate to Don
Quixote, Sancho and his ass, to write of the acts of
extravagant welcome performed in honour of the Englishman, I do not think that Góngora meant anything more
than to gibe Cervantes for the liberality he had always
shown in writing of those who were the enemies of his
country and of his faith. On the strength of this sonnet,
however, and without any other evidence, the Spanish
biographers have concluded that the official account,
which is extant, of the Earl of Nottingham's coming and
reception was actually written by Cervantes. On this
supposition, with a surprising lack of common judgment,
Hartzenbusch, the leading Cervantist critic and editor,
has included the *Relacion de las Fiestas de Valladolid*
among Cervantes' works in his magnificent edition of
Argamasilla. I confess I can see no trace of Cervantes'
hand—and it is impossible to mistake that hand, at least
in prose—in this dull, frigid, and lifeless composition.
Nor is it likely that a man in Cervantes' position, without
favour at Court, could have been employed in such a
work. Góngora's insinuation was like himself, mis-
chievous and malicious. There is another sonnet
printed by Pellicer, in truncated verse like those at
the beginning of *Don Quixote*, bitterly abusive of Lope

de Vega, which doubtless was also by Góngora, who hated Lope as much as he envied Cervantes, and probably thought by this stroke to take a double revenge. That this sonnet was, at the time at least, supposed by Lope to be the work of Cervantes is proved by a filthy and scurrilous sonnet in reply, attributed to Lope, in which Cervantes is furiously assailed. I have very little doubt that Góngora wrote both sonnets, with the object of setting his two enemies at each other.[1]

About this time there fell upon Cervantes and his modest household another trouble, involving doubtless a passing scandal, out of an occurrence which reads like a scene out of one of the comedies " of the cloak and sword." On a night in June 1605, Don Gaspar de Ezpeleta, one of the Court gallants, passing along the street where Cervantes lived — it is now the *Calle de Rastro*—was suddenly assailed by a man out of the darkness, who dealt him two severe blows and fled. Don Gaspar crying out for help, there ran to his succour the dwellers in the house near where he fell, among whom were Miguel de Cervantes and some of the women of his family. The wounded man was taken into Cervantes' apartments, where he died within a few hours, living long enough to bequeath some of his fine clothes to one of the ladies of the family in recognition of her services in attending to his hurts. In accordance with the rude custom of Spanish law, Cervantes and his family were taken off to the gaol, where they were detained until after the inquiry into the cause of Ezpeleta's death. The

---

[1] See the two sonnets, which are too vile for publication in this day, in Pellicer's *Life of Cervantes*, p. 110.

depositions before the Alcalde are still preserved, and
from them we glean some interesting particulars of Cervantes' mode of life at this period. The family of
Cervantes—himself fifty-seven years of age—consisted at
this time of Catalina, his wife; his natural daughter Isabel,
aged twenty ; his widowed sister Andrea, aged sixty-one;
her daughter Constanza, aged twenty-eight ; Magdalena
de Sotomayor, called Cervantes' sister—who must have
been a cousin—over forty ; with Maria, their servant.
Out of the depositions of the witnesses—that is, of the
members of the family themselves—we gather these
facts : that the household was poor, living in a house
shared by other tenants, in a not very fashionable quarter;
that Miguel de Cervantes had many visitors ; that he
"wrote and transacted affairs" there (*escribia y trataba
negocios*); and that the family, helped by some needlework
of the women, were dependent on him for their living.
There is no trace of any imputation upon Cervantes or
upon any member of this family arising out of this
unpleasant business. One of the witnesses, indeed, speaks
of a woman as having been the cause of the trouble—which
is probable enough, without witnesses. Don Gaspar de
Ezpeleta had a reputation for gallantry. In connection
with this story may be here mentioned another scandal
which my friend Don Pascual de Gayangos thinks he has
discovered, attaching to the name of Cervantes. There
is in the library of the British Museum a manuscript
diary by a Portuguese gentleman without name, living
about this time in Valladolid, apparently a loose liver
and given to gaming. In this diary the name of "Cervantes" once occurs in a not very reputable connection,
being uttered by a woman in a gambling house. But

Cervantes was not an uncommon name in Spain. There was another Miguel de Cervantes Saavedra, as I have shown, then living. With all deference to Señor Gayangos, I cannot but regret that without any other grounds than that of a name uttered by an anonymous Portuguese he should seem to suggest that our Miguel de Cervantes (now nearly sixty years of age) was a night-ruffler and a frequenter of gambling houses. Had there been any imputation on Cervantes' character we may be sure that we should have heard it repeated from the mouths of some of his enemies. But even the most venomous of them, he who wrote afterwards as Avellaneda, though he alludes maliciously to Cervantes' frequent imprisonments, never charges him with any crime worse than old age, infirmity, and depreciation of Lope de Vega.

In 1606 Philip III. moved the Court back to Madrid, whither Cervantes followed, apparently not yet having lost the hope of preferment in the king's service. Before settling in Madrid there is reason to believe, upon the strength of a certain manuscript discovered in 1864 by Señor Guerra y Orbe, in the Colombina Library of Seville, that Cervantes paid a flying visit to that city. Among the documents then discovered is one dating from the early part of the seventeenth century, containing among various pieces of humour by Quevedo and others, besides *La Tia Fingida*, a novel ascribed to Cervantes, an account of a burlesque tourney or poets' frolic held at San Juan de Alfarache, a village near Seville, in July 1606. Poems were recited, comedies acted in the open air, and a tournament fought with swords and spears. A narrative of the proceedings, in the shape of a letter to one Diego de Astudillo in the city of Seville, was written by some one whose name is not disclosed, who acted as secretary of the revels. From internal evidence there is strong reason to believe that this secretary was Miguel de Cervantes. The spirit and the style are his. The letter abounds in phrases such as occur in *Don Quixote*, with numerous allusions to the characters and incidents in the story. The burlesque names assumed by the competitors (among whom was Alarcon, the Mexican playwright) are clearly from the same mint as *Brandabarbaran de Boliche* and *Penta-polin the Garamantan.* I take this to be one of the "stray pieces going hereabout without the knowledge of their author," of which Cervantes speaks in his prologue to the Novels. In any case the tract is important as a literary document, showing that even at this early date, a year after its first publication, the names, phrases, and characters out of *Don Quixote* had become familiar in the mouths of the gay youth of the period.

The two chief patrons of Cervantes at this time were the Conde de Lemos, nephew and son-in-law of the reigning favourite, the Duke of Lerma, and Don Bernardo Sandoval y Rojas, archbishop of Toledo, who was of the same family, being uncle to the duke. Both these eminent men were noted for their fondness for learning and literature, and their liberality to poets and men of letters. The Conde de Lemos was President of the Council of the Indies, one of the highest offices in the State, which he exchanged in 1610 for the Vice-Royalty of Naples. He seems to have held out some promise of a place to Cervantes, but the brothers Argensola, Bartolomé and Lupercio, kept a monopoly of the Count's patronage, and though they pretended to be friends of Cervantes, they are suspected of having intercepted, as Cervantes himself hints, the Conde de Lemos's favour. In the third chapter of the *Voyage to Parnassus* there is a reference to promises made and expectations raised but unfulfilled, through "new occupations which had caused them to forget the pledges they had given." The Argensolas were old friends of Cervantes, of whom he had spoken very handsomely in several of his writings, especially in *Don Quixote*, where Lupercio Argensola's three plays were exalted above any of Lope de Vega's.[1] The Conde de Lemos, when at Naples, founded a literary society called the *Academia degli Oziosi*, under the direction of the Argensolas. Cervantes seems to have been disappointed that he was not asked to join the *Oziosi*. Perhaps it was well for his fame that he was not. Here, as in other instances of his life, it was the ingratitude of friends and the unkindness of patrons which proved to the advantage of the world. The Archbishop Sandoval, to whom, according to my belief, Cervantes owed a great deal, was, by his double position as head of the Spanish Church and Inquisitor-General, the most powerful ecclesiastic in Christendom next to the Pope. He was celebrated for his goodness of heart, his generosity, and his tolerance, and by various passages in his life he proved that he was a prelate in advance of his age. He twice refused the office of Inquisitor-General, and was only induced to accept it at last through a conviction that by holding it he might be able to investigate what Bossuet calls the "holy severities" of the Church. He is known to have

---

[1] See *Don Quixote*, Part. I., chap. xlviii.

S

discouraged the national taste for *autos-de-fé*, which were fewer under his administration than under any previous Inquisitor-General. He rebuked the Provincial Boards of the Inquisition for their over-zeal in witch-finding. A crowning proof of Archbishop Sandoval's enlightenment and liberality was shown in his taking Cervantes into his favour and extending his protection to that suspected book *Don Quixote*. That Cervantes was greatly indebted to the Archbishop's patronage for what I cannot but consider his singular immunity from the attentions of the Inquisition cannot be doubted, I think, by any one who has studied the history of those times; though the Spanish biographers, up to quite a recent date, have chosen to observe a conspiracy of silence on this and other points of our hero's career. How much the book owed to the Archbishop's favour is sufficiently proved by one fact. Both the First and the Second Parts were published not only without a word of notice from the Holy Office—which was a most unusual circumstance attending any publication of this character—but with the special approbation of the Archbishop of Toledo. Yet at Lisbon, which was outside of the Archbishop's jurisdiction, and where his authority as Inquisitor-General was probably of small force, there were some twenty passages in the First Part of *Don Quixote* which were marked as offensive to the Catholic Faith and ordered to be expunged. Nor was it until 1619, when both author and patron were dead, that the Central Holy Office, under a new Inquisitor-General, found anything offensive to true religion in *Don Quixote*.

There is reason to believe that, according to the

custom of the age, the favour received by Cervantes
from his patrons took the shape of gifts of money,
though it was not until some time after he had acquired
fame by *Don Quixote* that he relinquished all hope of
employment in the public service. In 1608 *Don Quixote*
reached what must be regarded as the true second
edition. The first had been printed, as we have said,
without the author's corrections. There was some excuse
for this, as Cervantes was then living at Valladolid. In
1608 the book was reprinted under his own eyes, and
various alterations and corrections of the text were made
which it is impossible to believe could have been made
by anybody but the author and by his authority. A
theory has been started by Hartzenbusch, himself the
most daring, careless, and irreverent—if not the most
incompetent—of editors, that even this second edition
of 1608 was corrected and amended by somebody other
than the author ; that Cervantes was so careless of his
most successful work as to let it take its chance a second
time with the printers ; that, having the opportunity of
correction and being on the spot to correct, he allowed
some other hand to revise and alter his book. This
theory would be unworthy of notice by me were it not
that it has been adopted and seriously defended by Mr.
John Ormsby, a competent Spanish scholar and very
capable critic, in his translation of *Don Quixote.* It is
sufficient to say that if we reject what has been the
belief of all the native authorities, including the Spanish
Academy, up to the time of Señor Hartzenbusch, we
must hold, not only that Cervantes valued the book
so little as not to care to revise his work when he had
the chance of so doing, but that he allowed material

alterations and additions to be made in the text by
some one who—seeing that on this theory he is the
author of Sancho Panza's lament over the loss of Dapple
—must have been of a genius not only akin but equal
to his own. Not more extravagant is the theory which
another modern translator has started, that Cervantes
purposely mutilated and defaced his story in order to
make it resemble the books of chivalry. What evidence
is there to show that Cervantes thought lightly of his
own work? In his Second Part we have abundant evidence to the contrary, showing Cervantes' sensitiveness
to his fame of author. It is true that he makes merry over
his blunders, but the very language he uses about them
proves that the subsequent corrections could have been
made by no hand but his own. The robbery of
Sancho's ass is precisely one of those passages over
which Cervantes indulges his humour, apparently at his
own expense, but really at the cost of his critics.
Had there been an independent and unauthorised corrector at work, is it possible that Cervantes, when
discussing this matter, should have passed him by
without at least a word of thanks? When Sancho
himself refers to the incident, and tells us of the trick by
which Ginés de Pasamonte stole his ass, how does he
conclude the story?—"The tears reached to my eyes,
and I s · up a lamentation which, if the author
of our history has not put in, you may reckon
he has not put in a good thing."[1] This story of
Sancho's ass and how it was stolen, and how he came to
be riding on it after it was stolen, was to the author

---

[1] See *Don Quixote*, Part II., chap. iv.

himself an infinite source of mirth, and would probably have diverted him more could he have foreseen how it would exercise his critics. The very fact that, in the edition of 1608, out of *seven* blunders about the ass which were in the edition of 1605, only *two* were corrected, seems to me conclusive that it was Cervantes himself and no other who was the corrector. Had the corrector been any other than the author he would surely have been set to do his task thoroughly. But it is highly characteristic of Cervantes that, while sensible of the blunder, he was too careless or too indolent to amend it entirely. There were other alterations in the text of 1608, which make it clear that it must have been revised by the author, so that we cannot be wrong in holding with the Spanish Academy of Letters, who based their own critical edition upon it, in regarding it as "the last choice of the author." It is quite as rare as any of the editions of 1605, and far more valuable.

CHAPTER X.

THERE is very little known of Cervantes' life in Madrid during the ten years which intervened between the first and second parts of *Don Quixote*. He seems, by various isolated passages and incidental allusions in his works, to have mixed with the best literary society then in the capital. He was a member, according to Navarrete, of a club called the *Selvages* (Savages), and paid and received the usual compliments between friends in the shape of commendatory sonnets, though we may imagine that, after the ridicule he had thrown on the practice in *Don Quixote*, some of those to whom the tributes were paid must have received them with a certain shyness. In 1609, being then in his sixty-second year, he sought to make a provision for his latter days and secure for himself decent burial by joining, according to the fashion of the age, a religious confraternity called the Order of the Knigh of Grace, of which order several of the leading men of letters as well as officials of the court were members, including Lope de Vega and Quevedo. His wife, and his sister and faithful companion Andrea (the latter of whom died in 1609), had already joined the Third (Lay) Order of St. Francis.

Encouraged, doubtless, by the fame he had acquired by his works, and especially by the popularity of *Don*

Quixote, Cervantes, whose genius had lain fallow for twenty years before this, began to collect his scattered writings, developing at the same time an activity and fecundity very remarkable in a man of his time of life. In 1613 he published for the first time his *Novelas Exemplares*—short stories of a kind then quite new, most of which had been written some years before. To turn them literally into *Exemplary Novels,* as our translators have done, is to convey a very hazy notion of what they were intended to be. They might better be called *Experimental Novels,* as in fact they were. Cervantes himself tells us that he chose to call them *Novelas Exemplares,* "because there is not one of them from which some profitable example (or instruction) cannot be drawn." In his prologue, which is as characteristic as all his prologues, sparkling with life and wit and good spirits, he claims to be "the first who has written novels in the Castilian tongue"—a claim which must be allowed, if by novels we mean connected short stories, dealing with real life and character. These are, in fact, the first attempts ever made in modern times in that kind of literature which has since flourished so luxuriantly. They are of various character and merit, exhibiting in an extraordinary degree not only the author's fertility of invention, but his deep and wide knowledge of life under many conditions. In a dedication to the Conde de Lemos Cervantes speaks with unusual bitterness of the evil tongues who, out of envy, tried to do him wrong, while offering to his patron thirteen (there were but twelve) of his tales, saying, "had they not been turned out of the workshop of my wit I might presume to place them by the best ever designed." This self-

complacency — always in Cervantes redeemed from
egotism by a subtle tone of humorous sincerity—was in
this case not without good warrant.   Although differing
greatly one from another in style, subject, and mode of
treatment, so that no two are alike in character, we can
hardly mistake the *Novelas* to be from any other than
the hand of Cervantes.   They may be classed as standing next in merit to *Don Quixote* among his prose
works, being esteemed indeed by native critics to be
superior in elegance and correctness of style.

   The English-Spanish Lady (*La Española Inglesa*) is a
charming, pathetic tale of a young girl who was taken
away by the English at the sacking of Cadiz by the Earl
of Essex in 1598.   Brought up in English ways by a
nobleman of Elizabeth's court, she is restored to her
parents and her faith ; and when on her way to the convent to become a novice, meets with her long-lost lover
in the person of a captive just freed from Algiers.   The
names and the characters of the English nobles—
Ricaredo, Arnesto, etc.—are amusingly unlike any types
of that nation.   Elizabeth herself and her courtiers
receive most delicate and generous treatment, such as
never in that age was extended to the enemy and the
heretic in Spain.   *Rinconete and Cortadillo* is also a
story of Seville, which may be taken to embody some of
Cervantes' experiences when at the lowest ebb of his
fortunes.   No such lively picture of the vagabond and
picaresque life has ever been painted.   It is as full of
colour and movement as Velasquez's *Borrachos*.   Monipodio is the literary father of *Fagin;* and the bullies
and cut-purses and troll-my-dames of his gang may have
furnished some hints to Scott for his Alsatia.   Next to

Don Quixote, Rinconete and Cortadillo must be reckoned
Cervantes' best piece of humour. *The Little Gipsy (La
Gitanilla)* is a beautiful and touching story, the founda-
tion of all the gipsy stories from that day to this, where
the heroine is a girl of noble parentage stolen by the
gitanos in infancy. Weber took his *libretto* of *Preciosa*,
as well as the name of his leading lady, from *La Gitanilla*,
which testifies to another side of Cervantes' profound
knowledge of Spanish Bohemian life. The ballads and
songs in this tale abound in tenderness and simple
pathos, and are among the best we have by Cervantes.
The Generous Lover (El Amante Liberal) takes us into
quite another sphere of the author's experiences, being
drawn from his own life as a captive in Algiers. It is
written in a style of somewhat redundant sentiment, in a
vein which recalls some of the episodes in *Don Quixote.*
*The Colloquy of the Two Dogs (Los Perros de Mahudes),
Scipio and Berganza,* is another reminiscence of the
Triana—a study of low life at Seville, where Monipodio
again figures. This and another of the tales, oddly
named *The Licentiate Glass-house (El Licenciado Vidriera),*
abound in dark allusions to matters of passing and local
interest now forgotten, and satirical touches of which
the point has been blunted by time. *The Licentiate
Glass-house* (which may almost be taken for the first
sketch of *Don Quixote*) is an eccentric scholar, whose
brain has been turned by a love-potion, who wanders
about the streets delivering himself of quaint enigmatical
speeches. *The Illustrious Scullery-Maid (La Ilustre
Fregona)* is one of the best constructed of the little
stories, truly an "examplar" for the simple and easy art
with which the *dénouement* is reached. The scene is

laid in a lodging-house of Toledo, which still survives as *La Posada de Sangre*, in almost the same state as when Constanza served there as scullery-maid. *The Jealous Estremaduran* (*El Zeloso Extremeño*) is a tale of intrigue and jealousy, written, like *The Deceitful Marriage* (*El Casamiento Erganoso*), in a lower key than most of the others. They are probably both of them founded on histories of real life. *The Two Damsels* are of a more romantic cast. *The Force of Blood* is an interesting and lively story; and so is *The Lady Cornelia*, which again is in a different style from any of the others. All of the Novels are distinguished, not only by a peculiar grace of style and delicacy of expression, which have made them classic in their own country, but for a certain force and sharpness of touch which prove them to have been drawn from real life, most likely from the author's personal experience.

The *Novelas Exemplares* were received with great favour by Cervantes' contemporaries—nay, among the literary cliques, with greater favour than *Don Quixote.* It was a kind of composition in which Cervantes had no rival or predecessor, success in which could give no offence. The name of "The Boccaccio of Spain," given him by the dramatist, Gabriel Tellez (better known as Tirso de Molina), was indeed not a very happy one, for the Novels are as different in style and treatment from the Italian tales as they are superior to them in art and in purity, both of taste and of touch. Even Lope de Vega, who followed Cervantes soon after in this line, as he had followed him in every other, was pleased to admit that they were not wanting "in grace and style." Ten editions were called for in nine years, showing that next after *Don Quixote* the most popular of Cervantes' works was the *Exemplary Novels.* By foreigners they have been unduly neglected, falling as they do, with all the other minor products of Cervantes' genius, under the shadow thrown across the ages by his towering masterpiece, *Don Quixote.*[1]

The year following, in 1614, Cervantes made a less happy hit by his poem, *The Voyage to Parnassus*, or as it should more properly be—the title of the original being *Viaje del Parnaso*—*A Tour in Parnassus.* It is a poem in eight chapters, written in *terza rima*, the idea as well as the title of which was borrowed by Cervantes —a debt acknowledged in the opening line—from the *Viaggio di Parnaso* of Cesare Caporali, an obscure Italian poet of the preceding generation. Except the leading idea, the title, and the metre (which last may be said to be common property), Cervantes has taken nothing from the Italian poet, who, with his works, is now forgotten. The chief interest of the *Voyage to Parnassus* is in its autobiographical details, which are fuller and more precise than any which Cervantes had yet given to the world. I cannot agree with Ticknor, however, who sees "little merit" in the poem. The leading idea—a battle between the good and bad poets—has been used since by Swift in his *Battle of the Books.* The bad poets having captured Parnassus, Apollo calls upon Cervantes to consult him as to who should

---

[1] The *Exemplary Novels* have never been adequately translated into English. There is a capital version, however, of six of them by James Mabbe (1640), somewhat extravagantly praised by Godwin as "perhaps the most perfect specimen of pure translation in the language."

be enlisted to drive out the intruders. Mercury is sent
on this mission in a galley built of allegory and rigged
with verse—a conceit which affords the author a capital
subject for the exercise of his powers of fancy and invention. Unhappily the occasion is also such a one as calls
out all his weaknesses—especially his excessive good-
nature, and that most uncommon of faults in a poet, an
over-weening estimate of the works of his friends. The
interminable roll-call of fifth-rate poetasters, most of
whom would have died but for this record, hardly
relieved by a passing stroke here and there of irony or
sarcasm, is a burden heavy enough to sink even a more
buoyant craft than that of Apollo's messenger—of which
the rigging is of *seguidillas*, the yards of couplets, and
the timbers of stanzas. Still there are scattered about
this uninviting poem many touches of grace and fancy,
which would be wonderful in an old man of sixty-seven,
were they not outdone by the proof of vigour still more
wonderful which he was soon to give. The chief value
of the *Voyage to Parnassus* lies in the third and fourth
chapters, in which the poet gives us a summary of his
own literary career, with pregnant hints as to his way of
life, his poverty and its causes. From these passages,
which are also among the pleasantest in the poem for
their gaiety and good humour, we learn some things
about Cervantes which are nowhere else to be found.

If for nothing else, the *Voyage to Parnassus* should be
precious to us for the Appendix or *Adjunta*, reading
which we are able to understand how it is that the booksellers of that age were of opinion, so naïvely repeated by
Cervantes himself, that "of his prose much was to be expected, but of his verse, nothing." This prose Appendix,

if only for the living figure of Pancracio de Roncesvalles, the young exquisite of the period with an ambition
to be poet, deserves to live among the best examples of
the peculiar Cervantic humour, with its mingling of grace,
wit, and high spirits. Not less delightful is the picture
which Cervantes gives us of himself and his occupations,
even introducing us within his house, which, we learn,
was at this time in the Calle de las Huertas, "facing the
houses where the Prince of Morocco used to live."[1] We
learn also how that his niece took in a letter, paying a
real for postage, which turned out to be a bad, dull
sonnet, without cleverness or point, in dispraise of *Don
Quixote;* and how that Cervantes himself had then six
comedies in hand, with as many farces, which he thought
of giving to the press, as the managers would not have
them, seeing that they had their own playwrights hanging
on them whom they were bound to employ. We learn,
among other things, that there were some poets who were
discontented with the notice which they received in the
Voyage to Parnassus. Among these was Manuel de
Villegas, the author of *Las Eroticas,* who, thinking that
his friend Bartolomé de Argensola had not been praised
enough, therefore assailed Cervantes as "a bad poet
and Quixotist"—Villegas, being himself a dependant
on the Conde de Lemos, and therefore not disinterested

---

[1] In June 1609 Cervantes was living in the Calle de la Magdalena,
soon afterwards moving to behind the college of N. S. de Loreto. In
June 1610 he occupied the house No. 9 in the Calle del Leon. In
1614, as we see above, he was living in the Calle de las Huertas,
returning to the Calle del Leon to No. 20, where he died. All
these sites in Madrid are to be now easily identified, though the
streets have changed names and the houses their numbers.

in the vilification of Cervantes and in the exalting of Argensola, the chief dispenser of his countship's bounties.

The new Comedies and Interludes which Cervantes spoke of in the *Adjunta a' Parnaso* were brought out the next year, eight of each in number. These, as has been said, had never been played, and there is much reason to doubt whether the Comedies at least were ever intended for representation. The Comedies are perhaps the worst of all the things that Cervantes ever wrote,— so bad that one Blas de Nasarre (the same foolish person, Navarrete declares, who wrote the misleading marginal note in the parish register of Alcázar[1]), who reprinted these plays in 1749, with the sinister intent (as Ticknor shrewdly surmises) of injuring the reputation of their author, gravely starts the theory that Cervantes made them purposely wild and irregular in order to caricature the plays of Lope de Vega, just as he had written *Don Quixote* to parody the old romances!—There is no kind of foolish or malicious invention from which Cervantes, during his life or after, has not suffered. Bad as these Comedies were, a bookseller was found to buy them, on the strength of Cervantes' reputation as a writer. Cervantes himself gives a perfectly modest and straightforward account of the transaction. " I sold them to the bookseller, who sent them to the press. He paid me a reasonable sum for them ; I took my money meekly, without making account of the quirks and quibbles of the players. I would they were the best in the world, or at least of fair worth." The Comedies are certainly not

---

[1] See *ante*, page 14.

good, the author violating in them every one of those excellent canons of art which he had himself laid down in the forty-eighth chapter of the First Part of *Don Quixote.* The Interludes, or Farces, however, are very much superior to the longer plays in spirit and in style. *The Watchful Guardian* (*La Guarda Cuidadosa*), where an old soldier is introduced as standing sentry over a house where his mistress lodges and keeping off his rivals by various tricks, is alive with comic humour—full of bustle and movement and of quips and cranks and *double-entendres,* such as might qualify it for a Palais Royal audience. Most of these shorter pieces have telling situations, with smartness of dialogue and rapidity of action, so that there is nothing to prevent them being acted now, if the taste and fashion of the age would allow.

During all this period of active production, or at least from 1612, as may be gathered from patent hints in his other works and palpable indications in the book itself, Cervantes was engaged in the completion of his great work by adding a Second Part to *Don Quixote.* That he did not originally contemplate a Second Part, but intended the first to be a perfect story in itself, is sufficiently indicated by his division of the original publication of 1605 into four parts, in imitation of the books of *Amadis.* That he afterwards changed his purpose and, even before the original *Don Quixote* was completed, had conceived the design of adding a Second Part, is distinctly proved by his own words, or by the words he has put into the mouth of Cid Hamet Benengeli, the presumed Arabic author. The very last sentence in the first *Don Quixote,* after the author has told us that certain verses relating to the knight had been delivered to a university scholar to be deciphered, goes on thus :—"We are informed that he has done so at the cost of many night vigils and much labour; and that he means to make them public, giving us the hope of the third sally of Don Quixote." I cannot see how any other meaning can be attached to these words than that Cervantes himself proposed some day to give the public an additional volume of the adventures of Don Quixote. Yet there are modern critics who pretend to discover evidence of Cervantes' indifference to the fate of his book in the concluding line from *Orlando Furioso*, with which he takes leave of his readers :—

" Forse altri canterà con miglior plettro."

M. Germond de Lavigne, an ingenious paradoxist of the school of Victor Hugo, who cherishes a curious antipathy to Cervantes, even interprets the line as an invitation to some one else to continue *Don Quixote*, holding that inasmuch as the original author had dismissed his hero in the same words as Ariosto had dismissed Medoro and Angelica, so he had parted for ever with his right in Don Quixote. In this interpretation I am sorry to find that the eccentric Frenchman has been followed by a sensible English writer and faithful Cervantist, Mr. Ormsby, who appears to be possessed with the notion that the sorrows of Cervantes have borne too deep an emphasis ; that he was not so badly treated as has been thought, even in that passage of life to which I shall presently come. Cervantes probably foresaw that what had happened to others would happen to himself—that some other person would venture to trade on the popularity of *Don Quixote* by bringing out a Second Part. But that he resigned his own right to do so is an extraordinary view to take of his character, and but a poor compliment to his insight. What does Cervantes himself say in the beginning of his own Second Part?—"And does the author, perchance, promise a Second Part?" inquired Don Quixote.—"Yes, he promises it," answered Samson Carrasco; "but he has not found it, nor does he know who has it; and so we are in doubt whether it will come out or not." This was written, let us remember, some time in 1612, before Cervantes had any reason to suspect any one else of venturing upon the task. Meanwhile the public had demanded a Second Part. "Let us have more Quixoteries; let Don Quixote fall to, and Sancho talk, and, come what will, we shall be content with that."[1]

[1] See *Don Quixote*, Part II., chap. iv.

CHAPTER XI.

WHILE Cervantes was engaged in completing the work which he must have felt to be his chief title to fame, the work to which his genius was called, for which it was specially fitted, there happened to him one of the severest crosses which he had yet encountered in his long life of misfortune. This, as the crowning incident of his literary career and a mystery in which is involved so much of personal and historical interest, it is necessary to dwell upon at some length. The blow was to be dealt him by a secret hand in his tenderest part. He had already announced, as we have seen, that he was occupied with the Second Part of *Don Quixote*. He had promised in his Prologue to the Novels that he would bring out "fast and speedily a continuation of the exploits of Don Quixote and the pleasantries of Sancho Panza." These words must have been written, as we gather from the date of the Dedication, about June 1613. Twelve months after, as we see by the date of Sancho's letter to his wife, Cervantes must have half written his Second Part. He was certainly known to be employed upon it ; and as we shall see afterwards, he must have communicated to some of his friends—the circle, perhaps, of the *Selvages*—some of the details of Don Quixote's third sally. Meanwhile there appeared, published at Tarragona in the summer of 1614, a book which claimed to be the "Second Part of the Ingenious Gentleman, Don Quixote," by the Licentiate Alonso de Fernandez de Avellaneda, native of Tordesillas. The work was dedicated to the "*Alcalde, regidors*, and *hidalgos* of the noble city of Argamasilla, happy country of the gentleman-knight, Don Quixote," etc. Dr. Rafael Orthoneda lent his approbation to the book as one which contained "nothing immodest or forbidden." The Vicar-General to the Archbishop of Tarragona gave a licence for the printing under his own hand, in terms which justify the suspicion, not only that the Vicar-General had a stomach for things immodest as strong as the Doctor Orthoneda, but that there was a kind of conspiracy among certain ecclesiastics to bring out the book with as much despatch and secrecy as possible, with a view to forestall Cervantes' own Second Part. That there was a deliberate purpose of fraud in this publication, apart from the malice contained within, is proved by the book being printed and got up so as to correspond with one of the two issues of the First Part, of Valencia, 1605. There can be no doubt that the printer of the spurious Second Part intended to pass it off as the true one, which had been publicly announced and was expected. As to Avellaneda, of course there was no such man. The native of Tordesillas remains to this day undiscovered, as discovered he would have been long ago had he been any common person. Of this audacious attempt to rob Cervantes of the glory of the authorship of *Don Quixote* —at least, to deprive him of the further fame and advantage he expected to derive from its continuation, it is impossible for the true Cervantist to speak with

patience.   Not every one is possessed of the courage or
the *sang-froid* of a modern English translator, who affects
to be angry with Cervantes for not bearing this blow more
meekly; who has himself fortitude enough almost to
forgive the audacious forestaller; who reproves the true
knight for showing temper towards the false one; who
is even of opinion that we owe a debt to Avellaneda,
seeing that but for him *Don Quixote* would have remained
"a mere *torso* instead of a complete work."[1]   But for
Avellaneda, Mr. Ormsby suggests, Cervantes would have
employed himself in other plans and projects—in turning
Don Quixote and Sancho into shepherds, so that "we
should never have made the acquaintance of the Duke
and Duchess, or gone with Sancho to Barataria."   But,
as I have already shown, Cervantes had finished more
than half the chapters of his Second Part, continuing
"the adventures of Don Quixote and the pleasantries
of Sancho," before he could have heard or dreamt of
Avellaneda.   In July 1612, two years before the publication of the spurious Second Part, the true author had
reached his thirty-sixth chapter.   By that time we had
already made the acquaintance of the Duke and Duchess,
and Sancho was already governor-elect of Barataria; so
that this service rendered by Avellaneda to Cervantes is
reduced to nothing.

On behalf of poor Cervantes it may be urged, in
mitigation of his offence in not bearing his injury with
greater fortitude (allowing that he lacked in anything
on this occasion which became a man of honour and
spirit), that no author before him had ever suffered as he

---

[1] See Mr. Ormsby's edition of *Don Quixote*, vol. i. p. 45.

did. It is true that of Mateo Aleman's book, *Guzman de Alfarache*, there had been also a spurious Second Part before Aleman brought out his own Second Part, but here the parallel ends. The continuator of *Guzman de Alfarache* did his work in no spirit hostile to the author. Though Aleman was quite as angry with him as Cervantes with Avellaneda, there is nothing to show that Juan Marti intended to degrade *Guzman de Alfarache*, still less to punish the author for writing it. There is not even anything to prove that Juan Marti knew of the design of Mateo Aleman to continue his own story. In the case of the *Don Quixote* we have positive evidence of the malicious intent of the writer who called himself Avellaneda. Imitators and continuators are not generally wanting in reverence for their author. They imitate a book because they think it good, nor in parodying it do they necessarily mean to degrade it, still less to hurt the author. Deliberately to spoil the characters and to abuse the story, while professing to revive them and to carry it on in the original spirit, without a thought of humour or any burlesque intention, merely out of spite to the author, this surely is what never was done before or since. In Avellaneda's Second Part we see not only a total insensibility to any feeling of romance or chivalry, but a studied contempt of Cervantes' design ; not only a brutal incapacity to apprehend the spirit of the book, but a malign intention to spoil the work because it is Cervantes'—to drag the story in the mire and besmirch it with filth. Avellaneda's Don Quixote is a common lunatic who is shut up in a madhouse, emerging therefrom when cured to become a mendicant, on whom Sancho bestows his charity. His Sancho is a vulgar glutton, a booby without sense or humour. For the witty and graceful Dorothea we have the foul drab Barbara. All grace, all tenderness, all flavour have vanished from the story, leaving as the residuum a dull, dirty, obscene book, which is a scandal on the literature of Spain.

The outrage on Cervantes would have been bad enough had it ended here. But in the Prologue we have nakedly revealed the true motive of the publication, which is to injure Cervantes in character, and despoil him, not only of the fame he had won by his *Don Quixote*, but of the profit he expected from the Second Part, the author thereby confessing that he knew there was a Second Part soon to be published. This Prologue, with its fierce and bitter tone of personal animosity, is a curiosity in literature—unmatched in any story of the quarrels of authors. Cervantes is reviled with a fury which, in its extravagance, becomes almost laughable. He is reproached not only for his faults as an author, but for the defects of his character and the infirmities of his body, even for his wounds, his old age, and his poverty. He is called "a cripple, a soldier old in years however youthful in spirits, envious, discontented, a back-biter, a malefactor, or at least a gaol-bird." He is likened in his ruined state to the old castle of San Cervantes. He is charged with having "more tongue than hands"—a double hit, of incredible malignity, at Cervantes' thickness of speech and to the hand disabled at Lepanto. In all the history of letters there is no such venom shown as Avellaneda pours upon Cervantes. He foams, he rages, he curses, till, like a drab, he has "unpacked his heart with words" and can blaspheme no more.

That even Cervantes' sweet nature was not wholly proof
against this last cowardly blow from an unseen hand
is evident enough from his Prologue to his own
Second Part, and from the frequent allusions to the
false pretender from this time forward in the true
Don Quixote. He seems to have first learned of
Avellaneda while writing his own fifty-ninth chapter.
Up to that point Cervantes had intended to carry his
hero to Zaragoza, to take part in the jousts which were
annually held in that city. As Avellaneda, however, had
forestalled him in this intention (which proves that the
writer, whoever he was, was informed of Cervantes' plans,
and probably had actually seen the original manuscript,
which he has copied in the outline and the letter in several
places), Cervantes, as he tells us himself, changed his
purpose, carrying the knight to Barcelona. Thence-
forward to the end of the book a constant stream of wit
and sarcasm is poured upon the false author and his
spurious inventions. There are some who have blamed
Cervantes for going out of his way to notice his adversary;
who pretend to think that the true *Quixote* has been
spoilt by the intrusion of the false image. He should
have dissembled his anger. He should have thought
more of his readers. He should have done this, he
should have done the other; being especially reproached
in that he was deficient in that property of "silent
contempt" in which critics are ever rich. M. Germond
de Lavigne, the apologist of Avellaneda, is even angered
with Cervantes that he did not welcome this *concurrent*
to his bosom, and reproaches him with lodging in his
soul *les petites passions de rivalité.*

All this appears to me to be very childish and most

ungrateful to Cervantes. He acted according to his nature—a nature which, we fear, fell short of the standard of the nineteenth century in philosophy. In his excuse, if he needs any, let it be urged that this was no common assault, of the sort which none knew so calmly how to bear. This masked enemy had struck his coward's blow with intent to spoil the one child of his genius which had thriven. A felon-knight, who dared not show his face or proclaim his name, had stolen across his path to filch from him the one glory which he might well believe to be destined for him—to rob him of the fruit of the great emprise which by all patent signs was reserved for him alone. A personal libel Cervantes was, of all men, best able to endure. His good nature, his forti-tude, his patience, had been tried and conclusively proved during a long life of unparalleled disaster. To taunt him with his age, his wounds, his infirmities, was but a clumsy malice, at which Cervantes might have been contented to laugh. To disparage his book, or rail at its success, was legitimate war, of which Cervantes could not complain. But this false *Don Quixote*, with its deliberate attempt to debase the work which it pretended to continue—to daub it with filth and trail it in the mud, with the view, openly avowed, of depriving the author of the profit which he expected from it—was an outrage which not even the magnanimous soul of Miguel de Cervantes could be expected to pass. Nor is there any good reason, I think, for his readers to complain of the manner in which Cervantes took his revenge. From his fifty-fourth chapter to the end he never lets go of his veiled antagonist, but pummels him with a skill and vigour which are not less surprising than the good humour and perfect coolness with which the punishment is inflicted. He seems even to take a boyish delight in the turning up of this unexpected chance of a good fight. His own *Don Quixote* was showing palpable signs of weariness. Adventures were almost exhausted. The plan of taking the knight to Zaragoza was not very promising. Even Sancho's spirits were beginning to flag. At this period there fell across Cervantes' way the new occasion of humour. The art with which he turns his assailant into his service —making of the forger an ally in passing off the true coinage, converting the enemy's steel into his whetstone, using the malicious intent for an aid to his own invention, and forcing the libeller's venom to heighten his own wit, with the perfect good humour and coolness with which he meets the unexpected assault—surely all this, whether from the artistic or the moral side, can never be praised enough. No less admirable, and even rarer, is the spirit of simple dignity and calm manliness in which he meets the attack which Avellaneda had made on his person and his character, in the Prologue to his own Second Part of *Don Quixote :*—" That which I cannot help feeling is that he charges me with being old and maimed, as though it had been in my power to stop time from passing over me, or as though my deformity had been produced in some tavern, and not in the grandest manner which ages past or present have seen or ages to come can hope to see. If my wounds do not shine in the eyes of him who looks on them, they are at least honoured in the estimation of those who know where they were acquired. For the soldier looks better dead in battle than safe and sound in flight. And

so much am I of this opinion, that if now I could devise
and bring about the impossible, I would rather be
present again in that wonderful action than now be
whole of my wounds, without having taken part therein.
Those the soldier shows in his face and in his breast are
stars which guide others to the heaven of honour and to
the coveting of praise deserved. And it should be considered that it is not with grey hairs one writes, but with
the understanding, which is wont to grow better with
years."

Nothing in Cervantes' life became him better than his
behaviour in this the occasion of his severest trial; and
indeed Avellaneda may almost be forgiven, as he is
forgotten, for he has helped to develop the work which
he tried to spoil, and to furnish us with fresh cause to
love and admire the man whom he slandered and tried
to wreck.

The inquiry as to who was Avellaneda is one which
we cannot avoid, even at the risk of dwelling too long
on this episode in the life of Cervantes—one of the most
curious chapters in the history of letters. The manner
in which the secret has been kept up to the present
time, in spite of all the attempts at piercing it, is itself
no small part of the mystery. That Avellaneda was an
assumed name is certain. No one of that name is
known to have lived and written in that age. The very
character of the book—its whole tone and style, even if
we could leave out the Prologue, where the malignant
motive is openly avowed—indicates that it was written
in no sincere spirit of authorship. So much is proved
by internal evidence as that Avellaneda was an Aragonese,
a Dominican monk, a writer of plays, and very intimate

with Lope de Vega, with a perfect knowledge of all that was in Lope's heart, and an extraordinary sympathy with Lope's feelings. That he was an Aragonese, Cervantes himself presumes, from his style, his dropping of the article before the noun, his use of the infinitive for the gerund, and certain other peculiarities for which the writers of Aragon are noted. That he was a monk is proved by his familiarity with monastic rules and observances and his frequent references to them. That he was a Dominican, and probably a preacher, was suspected by his profuse display of ecclesiastical lore, his quotations from the Fathers, and his partiality for the Dominican order. That he was a writer of comedies is evident from the personal offence he owns to taking at Cervantes' criticisms of the drama. Lastly, that he was one of Lope de Vega's very intimate friends—one who knew him almost as well as Murdoch Campbell knew the Marquis of Argyll, in Scott's legend—is clear from his making it a capital offence against Cervantes— in fact, charging upon Cervantes as the crown and sum of his iniquities—that in *Don Quixote* he had treated Lope de Vega with scant reverence—him, a holy person, a Familiar of the Inquisition.

The theories as to the authorship of the false *Don Quixote* are innumerable, and to deal with them at large would furnish a volume. Among the persons suspected, with more or less plausibility, are Luis de Aliaga, the King's Confessor, who succeeded the good Archbishop Sandoval as Inquisitor-General, and in that capacity made himself odious to the nation ; Bartolomé de Argensola, whom we have mentioned already as one of the friends who had failed Cervantes, whose claims are

favoured by M. Germond de Lavigne, Avellaneda's
eccentric defender ; Andrés Perez, the foul-minded
Dominican, who, under the pseudonym of Lopez de
Ubeda, wrote the dull and dirty *Picara Justina ;*
Alarcon, the dramatist ; Blanco de Paz, Cervantes' old
enemy of Algiers ; besides others of more or less note.
All these may be dismissed as failing in some essential
conditions. Aliaga has the strongest case, as being one
who bore the nickname of *Sancho Panza* among his
contemporaries, who must therefore have hated Cervantes and his invention. But then Aliaga hated
everybody of the literary profession, and was cordially
hated and ridiculed by them in return. There is a
curious passage in one of the last chapters of the Second
Part of *Don Quixote,* where, in the description of the
Knight's entrance into Barcelona, it is related that some
wicked boys of the city lifted the tails of Rozinante and
Dapple, and stuck under them branches of furze,
aliagas. This might have been intended as a sly hit at
Aliaga, but it is scarcely a proof that Cervantes took him
to be Avellaneda. I cannot believe that a person so
eminent and powerful as the King's Confessor, who had
been selected for that office by the Duke of Lerma, would
have condescended to employ himself in writing a continuation of *Don Quixote.* To him, as to all the others
whom the Spaniards have named, there is this fatal
objection, that none of them is proved to have had any
personal grudge against Cervantes on account of *Don
Quixote.* Who, then, could have been the secret enemy
who dealt Cervantes this foul blow? Who had motive
enough to hate him, and cause enough to resent his
success? Who had interest enough with archbishops and

the higher clergy to get his book published with their approbation? Who had his own personal reasons for degrading Cervantes' work and destroying his influence? It is curious that the hunt after a clue to Avellaneda, so eagerly kept up in Spain until quite lately, has slackened of late years, just when the search was getting "warm." I cannot help suspecting that the native critics have lost their zest for the search since it has dawned upon them that perhaps they might find too much. There is but one name which remains to be mentioned among those likely to have written the spurious *Don Quixote*, which good Spaniards seem afraid to utter. Some hints, indeed, have from the first been dropped that when the mask was lifted from Avellaneda it might disclose the features of the "Phœnix of the Age" himself—the great Lope, the lifelong rival and competitor of Cervantes—Lope de Vega, who was noted for his hatred and jealousy of all who came near his throne ; whom his own pupil and familiar friend called "the universal envier of the praises given to others."[1] No one had so strong a ground of complaint against *Don Quixote* as Lope de Vega. We have seen that he took the very earliest opportunity of disparaging the book. Even before it was published, he wrote to the Duke of Sesa, his patron, that "there was none so bad (poets) as Cervantes, or so stupid as to praise *Don Quixote*."[2] Lope de Vega might well imagine that *Don Quixote* was written specially against him, his

[1] Alarcon, the dramatist, who spoke of Lope as
    Envidioso universal
    De los aplausos agenos.

[2] The German, A. F. von Schack, who had access to the private papers of the representative of the Dukes of Sesa, was the first to bring this letter to the light in his *History of Dramatic Literature*

school, his profession, his influence. There was the Prologue, wherein he was assailed with merciless ridicule for his weaknesses and extravagances, his literary tricks and conceits; and there were the Prefatory verses, which made open mock of his own. There was that forty-eighth chapter in which the Canon of Toledo has the temerity to handle his comedies freely, and to denounce him as the chief of those who degraded the dramatic art by pandering to the tastes of the vulgar. Nay, the whole tenor and purpose of *Don Quixote* were, directly and indirectly, to bring discredit and contempt on all that was sacred in Lope's eyes and in the eyes of his patrons.

On the part of Cervantes there is no evidence of the existence of any feeling of enmity to Lope de Vega, though it may be that he was sometimes tempted to repine at a dispensation which placed a man whom he could not regard as his superior, who had entered the arena after him but had outrun him in the race, in a position so far above his own in worldly esteem and in fortune. In that bitter struggle for existence, however, I am not aware of a single act or word of Cervantes which is inconsistent with a friendly disposition towards Lope, and a generous recognition of his powers. No one had spoken so warmly and profusely in favour of Lope de Vega. So early as 1584, when Lope was a youth of twenty-two and yet unknown, Cervantes had named him as one of the rising poets of Spain and pro- phesied his greatness, in the *Canto de Caliope.* In 1598, when he was himself in his greatest misery, he had

and Art in Spain. It is believed that there are other papers still more compromising to Lope, preserved in private collections in Spain, which, from patriotic motives, their owners will not publish.

written a laudatory sonnet for Lope's *Dragontea.* In the First Part of *Don Quixote*, whenever Lope is directly mentioned, it is with abundant honour. In the forty-fifth chapter the Canon refers to "the infinite number of plays composed by a most happy genius of these kingdoms with so much glory, with so much grace, such elegant verse, such choice language, with such weighty sentiment,—finally, so rich in eloquence and loftiness of style, that the world is filled by his renown." Sometimes it may be that Cervantes spoke with his tongue in his cheek, echoing rather the popular voice than his own opinion, as when he quoted *La Ingratitud Vengada* as a specimen of plays that "sundry intelligent poets have written for their fame and renown,"—this being one of the most absurd and filthy of all Lope's comedies—a picture in which, according to Clemencin, is painted nothing but *imundicia y estiercol.* Ticknor observes, what is quite true, that in what Cervantes says of Lope de Vega there is "a tone of dignified reserve and caution." There could not be much love between men of natures so dissimilar. But even in the Prologue to the Second Part, when answering the accusation of Avellaneda that he had spoken lightly of "one whom nations the most remote so justly honour, and to whom our country owes so much for his innumerable stupendous comedies, written with all the vigour of art which the world demands, and with the correctness and purity to be expected from a minister of the Holy Office" (as if the Holy Office were guardians of the literary art as well as of the Faith)—Cervantes protests that he admires Lope's works and genius, and "his application continuous and virtuous."

On the other hand, it can be shown that Lope followed every step that Cervantes took in the path to literary fame, with a jealous persistence of which I know no example in the history of letters. Cervantes wrote *Galatea*, a pastoral ; Lope wrote *Dorotea*, a pastoral ; in close imitation of his model. Cervantes wrote plays ; Lope wrote plays—here, by sheer force of productiveness, jostling his rival from the field. Cervantes wrote *Novels ;* Lope wrote *Novels*. Then Cervantes wrote *Don Quixote ;* and here Lope's instinct must have told him there was something he could not copy—which he had therefore better crush before it put out Lope de Vega and his art. Before this date, in return for all the other's frequent and profuse eulogies, he had only mentioned Cervantes twice during his lifetime, and then slightingly, in the preface to *Dorotea*. After Cervantes' death not one word was ever said by Lope in praise of *Don Quixote*. In the *Laurel de Apolo*, published four-teen years after Cervantes' death, there are some lines of what Ticknor calls "cold punning eulogy" of him, but only as a poet. In one of his later plays, *Amar sin .Saber á Quien*, there is a passing reference to *Don Quixote*, which "may God Cervantes pardon." No fur-ther evidence need be cited out of the mass of testimony which, if it were worth while, I might adduce to prove that Lope de Vega had no friendly feeling for Cervantes —that he regarded *Don Quixote* as a personal offence, and made war against it from its first appearance. No one, as I think I have shown, had so powerful a com-bination of motives for injuring Cervantes through his *Don Quixote*. As a priest, who detected that the book boded his order no good ; as a familiar of the Inquisition, which holy system had been brought to shame, or at least made subject for laughter; as a writer, whose works had been held up to ridicule; as a dramatist, whose plays had been condemned; lastly, as the leading star of the literary firmament, whose lustre was threatened with eclipse, it was Lope de Vega who, of all men then living, was most likely to have written, singly or in collaboration, by his own hand or by another's, the false *Don Quixote.* No direct testimony will perhaps ever be forthcoming to clear up this mystery of Avellaneda; but the weight of evidence clearly indicates Lope de Vega as the man who dealt Cervantes this craven blow. I believe Cervantes himself suspected it, if he did not know it; and that this is the true explanation of the extraordinary zest with which he fell upon the book as matter for his own and his readers' entertainment.

This chapter would be incomplete if we did not record the fact, which seems to be a fitting appendix to this story of revenge and imposture, that not only has Avellaneda been justified in his act by certain critics, native and foreign, but even with Cervantes' own Second Part before them, there have been some who, from the first, have preferred the imitation to the original—the coarse burlesque, with its venomous intent, to the pure work of the true man—the base coinage to the sterling metal. Just as Shakespeare had his Greene and his Rymer, so Cervantes has his Lesage and his Lavigne. Although at the coming of the true Second Part the false one went out and was no more read, an attempt was made to resuscitate it during the reign of Philip V., the first of the Bourbons—an emanation, it is said, of the *Afrancesado* spirit, then dominant, which thought to find its interest

10

in depreciating the literary glories of the Golden Age of Spain. In 1732 Avellaneda was reprinted, with a preface by Blas de Nasarre (a foolish person of whom we have heard before), disguised under the name of Isidro Perales, declaring that the false Sancho was more natural than the real one; charging Cervantes with having borrowed his Second Part from Avellaneda, and averring that the glory of the veiled second author was the greater, for the droll reason that "it needs more force of genius to add to first inventions than to make them." Don Agustin Montiano, secretary to King Philip V., in giving his approbation to the work, reproaches Cervantes for his harsh remarks on his competitor, defends Avellaneda from the charge of being "cold and without mirth," and does not believe that any judicious man would decide in favour of Cervantes. A greater than any of these false Spaniards, sad to say even Le Sage—who probably eyed *Don Quixote* with the same disfavour as a small pirate might regard a rich argosy too strong to plunder—gave Avellaneda an elegant French dress, trimming and combing him out of all Spanish character, omitting the barbarities and all of the bawdry which was merely gross, and could not be made piquant. According to this judge of what was knightly and romantic, "Avellaneda has very well sustained the character of Don Quixote; he has made a knight-errant who is always grave, and all whose words are magnificent, pompous, and flowery." The latest of this sect of odd, perverse antipathists, who may be said to hold the same place in regard to Cervantes as the disciples of the mad Delia Bacon do to Shakespeare, is M. Germond de Lavigne—an ingenious Frenchman, who grudges Spain its glory in Cervantes. He has taken up the cause of Avellaneda with singular warmth, and abuses everybody who prefers the original *Don Quixote* to the imitation. He has translated Avellaneda afresh (with the bad parts left out), and in an elaborate introduction, full of undisciplined scholarship and misdirected energy, maintains its superiority. He denies the grossness of Avellaneda and the delicacy of Cervantes; insists that the copyist is entitled to our respect by reason of his strict attention to "the logical succession of the master's ideas;" with a sublime audacity charges Cervantes with plagiarism from his imitator; finally, pronounces sentence on Cervantes, "*un esprit léger, frivole, et vagabond !*"

It is not easy to go beyond this; but Spain herself may claim to have done so, in admitting Avellaneda's work among the classics of the language—a place being found in the *Biblioteca de los Autores Españoles*—the only collection of the national literature—for the false *Don Quixote* by the side of the true one.

CHAPTER XII.

ABOUT the time that his enemy's book reached him Cervantes was engaged, with other of the leading poets of the age, to write an ode in honour of the nun Teresa, on the occasion of her beatification by Pope Paul V., which poem was printed the next year among the select ones, and is as good as any of them—which is no great praise. In July 1615, in the dedication of his new Comedies to the Conde de Lemos, Cervantes speaks of Don Quixote as "waiting in the Second Part, booted and spurred, to do him homage." The Approbation prefixed to the Second Part was already written in February of this year by Marquéz Torres, the Archbishop of Toledo's chaplain, and is deserving of particular attention as expressing the opinion of a cultivated man of that age (who probably spoke the sentiments of his master the Archbishop) upon the works of Cervantes, and containing a very interesting anecdote about the author, his condition of life, and fame in foreign countries. After speaking in terms of unusual warmth of Cervantes' genius and character, and informing us that his works had already become known and esteemed not only throughout all Spain, but in France, Italy, Germany, and Flanders, the excellent Torres goes on to tell this capital story, which, strangely enough, is nearly always omitted in the English translations of *Don Quixote:*—

"On the 25th of February in this year 1615, the very
illustrious Don Bernardo de Sandoval y Rojas, Cardinal-
Archbishop of Toledo, my master, having gone to return
a visit which the Ambassador of France[1] had made to
his Excellency, who had come to treat of the marriage
of his Princes with those of Spain, several French gentlemen of those who came in the suite of the Ambassador,
as courteous as intelligent, and fond of polite letters,
came up to me and other chaplains of the Cardinal, my
lord, desiring to know what books of most worth were
current; and touching by chance on this which I was
then examining, scarce did they hear the name of *Miguel
de Cervantes* when they began to wag their tongues
(*hacer lenguas*), expatiating on the estimation in which
his works were held, not only in France but the
neighbouring countries—the *Galatea*, which one of
them had almost by heart, the First Part of this
(*Don Quixote*), and the *Novels.* Their commendations
ran so high that I offered to take them where they
might see the author, which offer they received with
a thousand demonstrations of lively eagerness. They
inquired very particularly as to his age, his pursuits, his
condition, and fortune. I was obliged to say that he
was an old man, a soldier, a gentleman, and poor; to
which one replied in these very words : 'But does not
Spain keep such a man rich, supported out of the public
exchequer?' Another of those gentlemen broke in with

---

[1] This was the Duc de Mayenne, called by Spanish writers the
Duque de Umena, who was sent by the Regent Anne of Austria
to conclude the double marriage of the Prince of Asturias (afterwards Philip IV.) with Isabelle de Bourbon, and of Louis XIII. with
the infanta Anna.

this sentiment, saying with much acuteness, 'If it is necessity obliges him to write, may God send he may never have abundance, so that, poor himself, he may enrich the whole world with his works.'" Marquéz Torres, whose mode of expression is a little clumsy, concludes by begging pardon of his readers for making his "approbation" so long, and trusts that they may not attribute the warmth of his eulogies of Miguel de Cervantes to any self-seeking motive, seeing that the homage is "not paid to one who is able to cram the mouth of the flatterer."

The licence to print the Second Part was not granted until November 5th, 1615; the dedication to the Conde de Lemos being dated the last day of October. Here the author speaks of his having made haste to publish, in order to be rid of "the disgust and nausea" which another Don Quixote had caused him. The publisher and printer of the Second Part were, as of the First, ten years before, Francisco de Robles and Juan de la Cuesta.

That Cervantes hurried over his last chapters, so as to be face to face with his adversary as quickly as possible, is obvious enough from many signs, but, except in turning his hero away from the road to Zaragoza to take that of Barcelona, and in the frequent digressions where the false Quixote and the false Sancho are assailed, always with excellent point, humour, and ingenuity, I do not perceive that he materially altered the scheme and course of his own Second Part. The *dénouement* is brought about in the sixty-fourth chapter, through the overthrow of the Knight of the Lions by the Knight of the White Moon, precisely as had been foreseen in Chapter XV. It was led up to from the beginning of

Don Quixote's third sally, and arranged with such entire
accordance with the laws of therapeutics, as well as of
chivalry, that an admiring medical critic, the Doctor
Morejon, has written a tract to prove that in his treatment of mental diseases by moral remedies the author
was the equal of Hippocrates and the precursor of Pinel.
And here I cannot help noting the strange blunder
which Heine has made in that delightful essay of his,
which proves him otherwise to be in full sympathy
with Cervantes, when he dwells upon the last scene of
overwhelming pathos, where the poor, prostrate knight,
with his adversary's lance at his throat, cries with a
feeble and broken voice to his conqueror, "Dulcinea del
Toboso is the most beautiful woman in the world, and
I the most unfortunate knight upon earth; and it is
not well that my weakness should discredit the truth.
Thrust home thy lance, knight, and rid me of life, since
thou hast bereft me of honour!" Surely there is no
scene more moving in all the range of romance, no
dénouement so true and perfect to any story or drama,
ancient and modern. But the remark of the romance-
master on this consummate finish to Cervantes' story is
unfortunate, in one who was all his life haunted as he
says by the shadow of Don Quixote and his squire:—
"Alas! this shining knight of the silver moon, who
overcame the bravest and noblest of men, was a
disguised barber!"—Alas, and alas, for the critic!
Cervantes knew his business better than this. The
Knight of the White Moon is no barber disguised, but
the scholar and the wit Samson Carrasco, who undertakes
this adventure, and, being such a character as he is, is
happily fitted for the enterprise. No other person in the

story would have been equal to the exploit, which for Master Nicholas to have attempted would have been to reduce the romance to buffoonery and degrade the pathos to burlesque. To cure the madman through the very means of his craze and to make the man of wit the healer—this was of the very essence of Cervantes' invention, the purpose of his story, steadily pursued to the end. Being cured, there was nothing else for Alonso Quixano, his wits being restored, than to die; and with his death was taken away, as his creator declares, all excuse for any other author than Cid Hamet Benengeli to "resuscitate him and write interminable histories of his deeds."

The Second Part of *Don Quixote* achieved as great a popularity as the first, and from the circumstances attending the publication, was probably welcomed with a peculiar zest by his friends and admirers. The attempt by another hand to spoil the work by continuing it in another spirit had proved a signal failure. And though the true author himself, through the mouth of Samson Carrasco, avers that "second parts were never good," he has been in this instance signally confuted. From that time to this the great majority of critics have agreed that the Second Part of *Don Quixote*, in the qualities that make the merits of a book, is better than the First. Charles Lamb is one of the lovers of Cervantes who is of a contrary opinion, averring that in "that unfortunate Second Part Cervantes sacrificed his instinct to his understanding." Lamb's grudge was chiefly against "the unworthy Duke and the most contemptible Duchess;" but to abuse them for the parts they are made to take is surely like Partridge at the play telling Queen Gertrude to "go about her business, for she is a vile, wicked wretch." The Duke and Duchess are created but as foils to Don Quixote, and their creator may be supposed to know what he intended. Who would give them up now, even though we are angry with the tricks they put upon their guest? Cervantes had need of them in order to enlarge the scene, and to exhibit his hero in his real calling. And who would be without Barataria, which Sancho would never have got without the Duke?—With all the mischief they work upon him, the Duke and Duchess are clearly meant to have an affection for the Knight, as their order had for the romances of chivalry which were chiefly composed for their pleasure.

That Cervantes changed the character of Don Quixote in his Second Part, and possibly altered the design and motive of his story, may be admitted. That he did so with any conscious sense of a change of purpose I do not believe. The pen of genius, as Heine says, is always greater than the writer himself. Don Quixote had grown since he was first conceived into a larger and purer nature. It is a process as delightful as it is natural, for which we ought not to blame Cervantes. Success in a line which was entirely new and more than perilous had made the author more daring in his second attempt. The First Part was an experiment in an untried field; in the Second there is no longer any doubt. The writer is on firmer ground, and sure of his purpose. The fable expands, as if from within; the characters are more fully developed; the action is quicker, larger, and more picturesque. The author has fallen in love with his own creations, and attends more carefully to their behaviour. Don Quixote

is less the man out of his wits, and more the man of
understanding.   Above all, there is a difference in
Sancho, who plays a more important part in the piece,
growing in humour and in wisdom, and improving in
his manners, so as to attract even Don Quixote's notice
to his improvement.   What can be more natural than
such a result of their association?   Sancho begins
by believing in Don Quixote's sincerity, being so
carried away by his master's superior nature, exhibited
even in his delusions, as to credit them in spite of the
evidence of his senses.   But he ends by imposing his
own deception on his master, as he takes a better
measure of the other's weakness, and makes him an
accomplice, through his imagination, in his impudent
tricks.   In all this the Second Part of *Don Quixote* is
but the legitimate and natural evolution from the First.
The new personages who are introduced, especially
Samson Carrasco, are not only interesting in themselves,
but necessary for the interest of the story.   One notable
difference between the First and the Second Parts is that
the parody of the old romances is, to a large extent,
dropped.   Don Quixote no longer attends to the copying
of Amadis.   There are fewer references to the books of
chivalries.   Indeed, we might almost imagine that Cervantes half repents of the effectual way in which he had
done his work of destroying those foolish but beloved
books.   His purpose accomplished, he sets himself to
provide the reader with an agreeable compensation.
Therefore he pours out all the resources of his genius
and his art in this Second Part.   Adventure flows from
adventure in an amazing succession.   There is a larger
invention; there is a firmer grasp of the story; there is,

lastly, more human nature in the Second Part than in the First. Something of a charm ineffable and unique must, of course, ever reside in an original book which its continuation must lack; and in this the First is better than the Second, because it is the First. But the story of the Second is better constructed, with more humour between the parts, with more freedom in the action, more skill in the development of the author's design. For the reader the flow of delight is not interrupted by those interminable episodes which Cervantes himself confessed to be a defect in his First Part. And if we have lost something in the Second Part; if Don Quixote becomes less romantic, the author more self-conscious, the story more artificial—is it no recompense to have gained the new Sancho with his vastly increased store of proverbs; the Governor of Barataria; the adventure of the Lions; the descent into the Cave of Montesinos; the flight of the Wooden Horse; Master Peter and his puppet-show; the scourging of Sancho; the letters of Sancho? There is, finally, the process of the disenchantment of Dulcinea, which fits the story with so perfect a motive, keeps up the interest just when it begins to flag, and rounds it off so naturally and easily.

The marvel of all this is that this book, with its frolic grace, its abundant wealth of humour and perpetual flow of life and invention; so rich in blood and overflowing with the sense of existence; so brimful of humanity, of love, and of hope; should be the work of a man approaching the seventieth year of a life of trouble, of toil, of privation, and of disappointment such as few men, and among them no great writer, ever lived. The completion of his great work preceded but by a few months the

close of Cervantes' career.   Yet his gay and bold spirit,
now rejoicing perhaps for the first time in that which is
the author's chief solace and delight, the sense of a
responsive and sympathetic circle of readers, was still
projecting new schemes of books.   In the dedication of
the Second Part of *Don Quixote*, Cervantes announced
to his patron that in four months his new romance,
Persiles and Sigismunda, would be ready, which was to
be "either the worst or the best of books of entertainment in our language."   He had spoken of the
Persiles two years before, in his prologue to the *Novels*,
as a book in which he was to enter into competition
with Heliodorus, and also of another work, *The Weeks
of the Garden* (*Las Semanas del Jardin*).   In the dedication of his *Comedies* he had referred again to "the
great *Persiles*," to the *Weeks of the Garden*, and to the
Second Part of *Galatea* (which had been spoken of in
the First Part of *Don Quixote*) as forthcoming, "if my
old shoulders can carry so heavy a burden."   Of these
projects the only one which Cervantes lived to carry out
was his romantic story of *Persiles and Sigismunda*, a
book of imaginary travels, after the style of Heliodorus,
though this was not published till after his death.   In the
prologue to the *Persiles* there is a charming story told, in
Cervantes' own style, of which it is a perfect model, of a
little adventure which happened to him when returning
from his wife's town, Esquivias, whither he had gone for
change of air, to Madrid.   This is so pleasant a sketch
of a cheerful old age, undimmed by time, care, or sick-
ness, that, often as it has been quoted, I cannot refrain
from repeating it, being the last picture of himself which
Cervantes gives us from his own hand :—

"As it fell out, beloved reader, coming one day, I and two friends of mine, from the famous town of Esquivias, famous for a thousand things—one, for its illustrious families, and another, for its most illustrious wines—I was aware of one who came spurring in great haste behind my back, wishing to come up with us—a wish to which he gave voice, calling out to us not to push on so fast. We waited for him, and there came up on a little she-ass a grey student, for in grey was he all attired—gaiters, shoes, and sword in brass-bound scabbard—a shining Walloon collar, with pleats of equal length, though, sooth to say, there were but two of them, for the collar kept continually falling to one side, and he catching it up with great care and pains to keep it straight. Coming up with us, said he: 'Sure, your worships are bound for some office or benefice at Court, since it is there that his most Illustrious Eminence of Toledo is, and His Majesty as well, seeing the rate at which you are travelling; and indeed my ass has won the prize for his pace more than once.' To which one of my companions replied: 'The nag of Señor Miguel de Cervantes is to blame for this, for he is a quick stepper.' Scarce had the student heard the name *Cervantes* when, alighting from his mount, his pad falling on one side, his valise on the other,—for in all this splendour was he travelling,—he made for me, and hastily seizing me by the left hand,[1] cried: 'Yes, yes! it is he of the maimed hand, safe enough, the all-famous, the merry writer, and indeed the joy of the Muses!' To me, who in these brief terms saw of my praises the

---

[1] Here is evidence that Cervantes had still a left hand remaining, though mutilated and deformed.

grand compass, it seemed discourteous not to respond
to them, so, embracing him round the neck, whereby I
made entire havoc of the collar, I said: 'This is a
mistake in which many friends from ignorance have
fallen. Sir, I am Cervantes, but not the joy of the
Muses nor any of the fine things your worship has said.
Regain your ass and mount, and let us travel together in
pleasant talk for the rest of our short journey.' The
polite student did so ; we reduced our speed a little,
and at a leisurely pace pursued our journey, in the
course of which my infirmity was touched upon. The
good student checked my mirth in a moment: 'This
malady is the dropsy, which not all the water of Ocean,
let it be ever so sweet-drinking, can cure. Let your
worship, Señor Cervantes, set bounds to your drink, not
forgetting to eat, for so, without other medicine, you will
do well.'—'That many have told me,' answered I ; 'but
I can no more give up drinking for pleasure than if I
had been born for nothing else. My life is slipping
away, and by the diary my pulse is keeping, which at
the latest will end its reckoning this coming Sunday, I
have to close my life's account. Your worship has come
to know me in a rude moment, since there is no time
for me to show my gratitude for the good-will you have
shown me.' By this time we reached the Toledo bridge,
whither I betook myself—he turning aside to take the
road to Segovia."

The narrative, so characteristic of the gay good
humour of Cervantes, even in the near prospect of
death, ends with a farewell to all that had made life
sweet to him : "Good-bye, humours ; good-bye, pleasant
fancies ; good-bye, merry friends, for I perceive I am

dying, in the wish to see you happy in the other life."

The readers of the best of biographies will remember the affecting scene in the library at Abbotsford when Lockhart read out this passage to Scott—always a great lover and admirer of Cervantes—then stricken like him with a mortal disease, and approaching the end of his heroic days of strenuous labour. "Sir Walter did not remember the passage, and desired me to find it out in the life by Pellicer, which was at hand, and translate it. I did so, and he listened with lively and pensive interest." Wordsworth was there, himself in his youth not unvisited by dreams from "the groves of chivalry," who had in visions

Harmonious tribute paid
To patient courage, and unblemished truth,
To firm devotion, zeal unquenchable.[1]

Allan, the historical painter, was one of the circle, and told Lockhart, as he relates, that he "remembered nothing he ever saw with so much sad pleasure as the attitudes and aspect of Scott and Wordsworth as the story went on."

The end was now approaching. Three weeks before his death, lying sick in his own house, Cervantes made profession of the Third Order of St. Francis, whose habit he had assumed at Alcalá in 1613. Too much emphasis has been laid on this act, which is evidence rather of poverty than of piety, proving only that Cervantes died as he had lived, in conformity with the faith of a true Spaniard. In that age it was not possible for a man to

---

[1] See the Introduction to the *Prelude.*

die decently, or at least to be sure of decent burial, who was not enrolled in one of the religious orders. To be a good Catholic was then identical with being a good Spaniard, and Cervantes did what every man of sense was bound to do, not dreaming to cheat God and "to be sure of Paradise," by passing disguised, according to the Miltonian sarcasm, in Franciscan weeds, but in obedience to what was then a universal rule of good dying, to secure for his bones in the only mannerly way a safe resting-place, and his family polite consideration. Of the desperate condition of his fortunes, even in those last days, when he had reached the top of his fame, and was a popular author, whose books sold as none up to that time ever did, we have sad evidence in the pathetic letter written to his true friend and kind patron the Archbishop of Toledo, dated the 26th of March 1616, which is the last piece of writing extant in Cervantes' hand, running thus in English :—

"My very Illustrious Lord,—A few days since I received your most Illustrious Lordship's letter, and with it new proofs of your bounty. If for the malady which affects me there could be any relief, the repeated marks of favour and protection which your Illustrious Person bestows on me would be sufficient to relieve me ; but indeed it increases so greatly that I think it will make an end of me, although not of my gratitude. The Lord God preserve you as the executor of saintly deeds, so that you may taste of the fruit of them there in his holy glory, as fervently desires your humble servant, who kisses your most exalted hand.

"Miguel de Cervantes Saavedra."

The letter, of which I have a facsimile before me, is written in a firm, clear hand, showing no sign of age. Three weeks after writing it, Cervantes, who was then on his death-bed, penned the last of his dedications—of *Persiles and Sigismunda*—to his other patron, the Conde de Lemos, then on his return to Spain from Naples. Even to this point his courage is unshaken, and his spirits "as moving delicate and full of life" as when in his prime of manhood. Quoting the words of an old poem, and turning them to fit his own case, "with one foot in the stirrup, waiting the call of Death," he tells the Count :—"Yesterday they gave me Extreme Unction, and to-day I am writing. The time is short ; my agonies increase ; my hopes diminish." He repeats his assurances of regard and love for his Excellency, and enlarges, like a prodigal as he is ever of good-nature, on the bounties of which he has been the recipient. His mind is still occupied with his books. If by a miracle he survives, he purposes to leave to the world as relics of himself his *Weeks of the Garden* (which never appeared); "the famous *Bernardo*" (now for the first time mentioned, and never heard of again) ; and the sequel to the *Galatea*—that first-born of his youth, ever tenderly loved, of which he knows the Count to be an admirer. And so, with a last prayer for God's blessing on him, he ends, on the 19th of April 1616. Four days afterwards he died ; as those who are curious in coincidences have noted, on the same day, the 23rd of April, as Shakespeare. But the dates are only nominally identical, seeing that England had not then adopted the calendar of Gregory. Shakespeare, a younger man by seventeen years, outlived Cervantes by some ten days.

Cervantes was borne to his humble grave "with his face uncovered," we are told, according to the Franciscan ceremonial. No ceremonies else are recorded as taking

II

place at his funeral. Thirty years afterwards, when Lope de Vega followed him—always more fortunate than his lifelong rival—he was attended to the grave by an immense crowd, three bishops officiating at the rites, grandees bearing his coffin, amidst the tears of the populace; the funeral an affair of state, which lasted over nine days. The circling wheel of Time has re-dressed the balance. To-day it is the fame of the author of *Don Quixote* which lives in every tongue, while the name of Lope, once, according to Cervantes himself, a synonym for all that is good, is little else than a literary tradition.

By Cervantes' will—lost by his countrymen like almost everything else which was a memorial of him—his wife Doña Catalina and the Licentiate Francisco Nuñez, a lodger in his house, were appointed executors, their only direction being that they were to bury him in the grave-yard of the Trinitarian Convent in the Calle del Humilladero. The choice of this spot is a touching proof of Cervantes' constant gratefulness to those who had re-deemed him from his captivity—the good Father Juan Gil, the Redemptorist, having been a Trinitarian. It was, moreover, of this religious house that Cervantes' only child Isabel was an inmate. In the same ground were interred afterwards his wife, who died in 1626, and this same daughter, and other members of the family. No stone or inscription marked the spot where the great writer was laid. In 1635 the Trinitarian sisters moved into another convent in the Calle de Cantaranas (Sing-Frogs Street), exhuming, as the custom was, the bones of all the members of their order and friends, and trans-porting them to their new abode. There, mixed with remains of the meaner kind, and undistinguishable from the others, now rest what is mortal of MIGUEL DE CERVANTES.

His grateful country has since set up a bust of him (modelled after the fancy portrait by Kent) with appropriate attributes in the façade of the Trinitarian Convent in the Calle de Cantaranas, with a suitable inscription. On the house which Cervantes last occupied and where he died, at the corner of the Calle de Leon, abutting on the Calle de Francos, there was affixed by order of Ferdinand VII., a trophy, with poetical and military devices, enclosing a medallion (also fancy) portrait— the Calle de Francos having been more lately renamed the *Calle de Cervantes.* These—with the mean and common-looking bronze statue by Solá in the Plaza de Cortes, where *El Manco de Lepanto* is portrayed with the conventional hooked nose, and a too conscious expression of success in hiding his maimed left hand under the folds of his cloak—make up the sum of all that Spain has contributed, in solid brass or stone, to the acknowledgment of her debt to Miguel de Cervantes.

The *Persiles and Sigismunda,* which occupied his last thoughts, was published by his widow in 1617, with an approbation signed Josef de Valdivieso, assuring the reader that "of the many books written by Cervantes none is more ingenious, more cultured, or more entertaining." But neither is it the best nor the worst book in the world, as the author himself had predicted. This child of his old age is a romance written in professed imitation of the *Theogenes and Chariclea* of Heliodorus, and equally extravagant and insipid ; in an elegant, refined, and graceful style, superior in correctness to that of *Don Quixote*, but so different from that book as to make it a wonder that one hand should have written them both. The *Persiles*, strange to say, is a reversion to much of that old, artificial type of romance which Cervantes himself had exploded. A pair of lovers, under disguised names, set out on their travels and meet with various adventures. They tell a great many stories, and have a great many told to them; and after encountering shipwreck, captivity, ravishment, and every kind of peril by land and sea, from robbers, pirates, savages, and *alguazils*, turn up at Rome, where the gentleman is proved to be heir of the "King of Thule," and the lady own daughter of the "Queen of Friesland." They are blessed by the Pope, and live happy and have a large and virtuous family.

By few but the most fervent of Cervantists can *Persiles* now be read, and these few find their chief reward in unexpected bits detached from the author's own experience—a fight with Algerine corsairs (probably a reminiscence of the *Sol*), a sarcastic reference to the *Alcalde* and *Regidors* of some town unnamed, which may be Argamasilla, and numerous stories, told with Cervantes' old art of *raconteur*, which are a fruitful mine which dramatists and story-tellers of all countries since, such as our English Fletcher, for one, in his *Custom of the Country*, have worked with profit.

CHAPTER XIII

TO the world Cervantes is a name for ever connected with *Don Quixote*. Book and author are so closely related that it is not possible to study them apart. Just as *Don Quixote* was the reflection of the man Cervantes, so it is in the record of the life of Cervantes that we may find the true interpretation of the story of *Don Quixote*. What need of a key to the mystery which has exercised a thousand pens, native and foreign—namely, the object with which *Don Quixote* was written—when we have before us the open chapter of the life of Cervantes? What need of any mystery at all, when the author so distinctly declares that his book is so clear that children, grown men, and greybeards equally love, comprehend, and enjoy it? Let those who insist upon a secret purpose, who will not believe the author in his express declaration that he meant only a book of entertainment, continue to hug their theories of a recondite inner meaning. That *Don Quixote* is a "satire" a great many are convinced—of the immortal herd of those who cannot conceive how any man should be guilty of humour and yet intend no malice. Charles V., Philip II., the Duke of Lerma, Ignatius Loyola, down to the recalcitrant cousin of Doña Catalina, and the crazy *hidalgo* of Argamasilla, these are among the originals whom the shrewder sort of interpreters, from the Jesuit

Rapin down to the late Consul Rawdon Brown, of Venice, have detected in Cervantes' story. Of such theories it is only needful to say that those who can suppose that Cervantes meant, in painting Don Quixote, to revenge himself on any enemy, are beyond the reach of conversion. Scarcely less extravagant have been some of the later theories, which aim at the exaltation of Cervantes' work, and are founded on the idea that *Don Quixote* is too lightly appraised as a mere book of humour. The excellent Lieutenant-Colonel of Engineers, Don Vicente de Los Rios—whose introductory "analysis" of *Don Quixote* is worthy of honour as being the first grave and formal recognition of Cervantes in Spain as a classic—declared that the author of *Don Quixote* had proposed to imitate Homer in his *Iliad*, and that he was guided by the same rules in framing his story as Virgil had been in his *Æneid*. Don Nicolas de Benjumea, in our days, has discovered in the *Don Quixote* "a vast and profound allegory"—the strife of the new spirit of the age with the past, the eternal combat between Ormuz and Ahriman, between Typhon and Osiris, etc. ; finding in Dulcinea "the soul of Quixano objectivised," the name being an exact anagram of *diña luce* (the divine light)—the *Dama Lux* of Guinicelli, the *Dama Filosofia* of Dante, together with Ariosto's Angelica, the Yseult of the Armorican legendists, etc. These extravagances, which recall some of the flights of the poor crazed knight himself, are paralleled by some of the things which have been said of the man Cervantes. That he was a Social Reformer ; that he was an Evangelist who came to preach a new dispensation, political and religious ; that he hid his zeal for Purity under the cloak of humour ; that he had "a mission," which for greater deception of the unrighteous he veiled from the curious eyes of the period, but ineffectually from sharper ones of the present day—what absurdity is too great to repel some of the critics? It remained for M. Germond de Lavigne, the champion of the spurious *Don Quixote*, to cap all these crazes, native and foreign—even the discovery of the ingenious priest of Toledo, Father Sbarbi, who makes Cervantes out to be a perfect theologian—by announcing that Cervantes was a member of the party of the Federal Republic.[1]

It is necessary for us to defend Cervantes against these imputations, for his countrymen have been as careless of his fame as a great author as he was himself. Not until a century and a half had passed after his death did Spain recognise the worth of *Don Quixote* as a book of anything more than passing entertainment. Although popular, as we have seen, from the first, and delighting the multitude as no book of the first class ever did, before or since, it was a long time before Spaniards could be got to acknowledge that the work of *El Manco de Lepanto* was a lasting honour to their country and to their literature. There is ample proof, in the careless style in which the book was printed, on vilest song-book paper, with wretched type and ghastly "sculptures," with even the title altered to suit the vulgar taste—that *Don Quixote* was regarded as little better than a chap-book—a collection of drolleries which even some good Spaniards regarded askance as scandalous, being a caricature of some of the prominent vices of the national character. A good deal of the sneaking kindness which was bestowed

---

[1] M. Lavigne wrote an essay to sustain this thesis in a Madrid newspaper, *La Discusion*, in 1868.

on the false *Quixote* of Avellaneda at the time, and is still extended to that vile, malicious libel in Spain, I have no doubt is to be accounted for by the spirit of exaggerated nationalism, which suspected Cervantes of laughing at his own country. There was a feeling, which the priestly caste were early to foment, that Cervantes had carried his victory too far, even over the old romantic books, which, after all, were very Spanish—that his real design was to ridicule the weaknesses and superstitions of his countrymen, of whose taste for rodomontade and extravagance the romances were a faithful reflex. When Blas de Nasarre reprinted Cervantes' unlucky budget of un-acted plays in 1749, an anonymcus poet expressed what I suspect was the prevailing feeling, especially among the persons of culture, in some lines of bitter reproach against Cervantes, whose work Spain was declared to have applauded, "not seeing the poison hidden among those flowers of wit." It was of Spanish honour that the author was "the executioner." He had made a mock of "the dreaded valour of Spain." He had vilipended her institutions. His book, going among strangers, had given them entertainment at the expense of the country. This was the cause, the poet wrote, why *Don Quixote* was so well received throughout Europe—reprinted and translated, adorned with pictures, worked into tapestry, moulded into sculpture, and engraven on stone. "Fools! in this mirror ye see yourselves. This is what ye are and have been." In the same vein writes one Zavaleta, the author of a book published anony-mously in 1750, in which, after a glowing eulogy of Lope de Vega and of Calderon, he launches out into a furious attack on *Don Quixote* on account of its unnational spirit. Foreigners, we are told here, relish and praise *Don Quixote*—a book "dry, poor, dreamy, and, in fine, directed but to declare to the world the fatuous valour of a frantic madman"—because they find in it a picture of the Spanish character, with its tendency to vainglorious-ness and fanfaronade. And this, of the man who had fought and bled at Lepanto—who had written *La Numancia!*

The feeling is not yet extinct in Spain, and perhaps we may detect it in the last outrage which has been paid to the author of *Don Quixote*—namely, the inclusion of Avellaneda's foul and malignant parody in the *Biblioteca de los Autores Españoles*, the collection of national litera-ture published by Rivadeneyra. Of late years, indeed, it must be acknowledged that there has been a revival of sympathy for Cervantes in Spain, which has even grown into a kind of worship, in which the chaunting is out of proportion to the offering. They have run wild over The Joy of the Muses, The Prince of Wits, The Maimed One of Lepanto, whom they neglected and nearly starved in his lifetime. Yet for all this tardy enthusiasm, which finds expression chiefly in ode and acrostic, in mutual congratulations on his birthday, and flowering speeches in his praise, the jealous champions of the national honour whom we have quoted were so far right as that it is indubitably true that the fame of *Don Quixote* was first made in foreign countries. It was not until the homage of the nations had been paid that Spaniards, or at least the cultured portion of them, discovered that they had produced a genius equal to the greatest. England may fairly claim the chief honour for the recognition of Cervantes as one of the world's great writers. England was the first to give him welcome—Shakespeare being yet alive—and an English dress. In English was *Don Quixote* first translated, in Shelton's rude but picturesque language, so that the author of *Hamlet* might have read *Don Quixote* before he died. England was also the first of all nations, Spain not excepted, to give the book a proper dress as became a classic, in Spanish, with a biography, hitherto wanting, of the author.[1] Lastly, England was the first of all nations to furnish *Don Quixote* with a commentary—that of the devout and laborious Bowles, which, much neglected at the time, has since been duly appreciated by Spanish scholars, who have never ceased to pay it homage by pilfering from it all the learning and much of the critical apparatus.

To criticise a book which has for more than two centuries and a half passed into a world's possession is a kind of impertinence. There is no kindred soul, among the many who have written upon *Don Quixote*, who has failed to pay tribute to the genius of Cervantes. Spirits the most diverse—the most finely touched and the solidest—from the manly and whole-souled Walter Scott, who found here a kindred nature and an inspiration, to Heine, arch-mocker and præ-romanticist, who bubbles with enthusiasm over this whom he falsely calls the anti-enthusiast ; from the great master of English wit, the transcendent anti-humanist, author of *Gulliver*, to the gentle Lamb, with whom Cervantes was a prime favourite; from the misty and mystic Coleridge to Sainte-Beuve, gracefulest of French workmen in the technics of criticism—the great writers of many

---

[1] The life by Mayans y Siscar appended to the magnificent edition of the text published in London, 1738.

countries have united in rendering homage to the work of Cervantes. Those who praise nothing else praise *Don Quixote;* and there are some among those who read it who read nothing else. As a product of man's wit, it must be pronounced supreme among the children of the imagination. And this is the essence of the wonderful feat that Cervantes has achieved, that upon a theme of passing interest he has written a book of perennial attraction and value. The book of Spain has become the common property of mankind. The prophecy of Cervantes himself has been more than fulfilled: "There shall be no nation nor tongue without a translation." Every language has its *Don Quixote*, as it has its Bible. This, indeed, has been well called the "Bible of Humanity." This child of Cervantes' genius has been received by adoption into every family of mankind. There is no language but has borrowed from it some of its vocabulary. Quixote, Rozinante, Sancho Panza, Dulcinea, Maritornes—they are words in every tongue. It has been said that *Don Quixote* is untranslatable, which is but to say that it retains its full flavour only in the original. But no book has been oftener translated, into a greater number of tongues. And this is the best proof of its original and unique goodness, that, however roughly treated by the translator, in the driest and baldest version, it never loses all its charm or ceases to be readable. The grace and the spirit which abide in the letter cannot be "done," of course, into any other language. The characteristic Cervantes' flavour—the delicate play of words—the ever-flowing under-current of humour—the subtle half-meanings and double-meanings—the charm which resides in the careless simplicity of the original—this no translator

can hope to preserve.   But all is not lost, even in those
ribald versions, like that of Motteux in English, which,
treating *Don Quixote* as a quarry of precious though
hidden ore, sought to invest it with "the humour of the
times"—sparing no pains to make him diverting—*pour
mettre ce vieux comique à la mode*, as dealt an old
French translator with Plautus.

What is not lost—can never be lost, is the art which
underlies this incomparable story—the interest which
grows with each succeeding adventure—the perpetual
flow of human nature—the healthy, open-air spirit of
life—the humour, which is closely interwoven with the
whole texture of the fable, with its lining of pathos.
The art, unlike anything in literature, is so consummate
as well as so original that we are apt to under-estimate
the greatness of the miracle which Cervantes wrought.
Who could predict a success for a book built of
materials so slight—born of a fancy which seemed so
evanescent?   A gentleman of La Mancha, whose wits
have been turned by the reading of romances of
chivalry, going about in quest of adventures in company
with a village boor through that unloveliest and least
romantic of regions—what was there here to provide
entertainment for all mankind for ages to come?   It
is difficult to imagine how, out of stuff so slender,
a work was to be made which is equally delightful
to the Englishman and the Frenchman, the Greek,
the Hungarian, the Dutchman, and the Pole.   The
secret of the perennial freshness of *Don Quixote* is
but partially revealed in the story itself.   The art, indeed,
is in its kind, exquisite.   As a mere story-teller, there is
none to be matched with Cervantes.   He is the best, as

he was the first, of all moderns in a kind of work more often attempted, perhaps, than any other. Of the invention, what is to be said which is not an echo of a thousand voices? Don Quixote and Sancho have been the models, singly and in association, which the world has never tired of copying. The "errant star of knighthood, made more tender by eclipse," is still the type of all true chivalry. The courtesy, the kindliness of heart, the simplicity, the dignity, the fine sense of honour and of truth—which shine through all his grotesque deeds and ignoble surroundings, which survive through all his buffetings, his reverses, his crazes, so that we never cease to love and are almost ashamed to pity him, make up a picture of "a very perfect gentle knight," such as lives for ever, to give the world assurance of what was in the soul of the old chivalry, after all the knights are laid in the dust and the romances dead and forgotten. Such a picture must have been drawn with the heart and not with the hand. To suppose that the painter drew it as a caricature of knighthood, or as a parody of some living man, or as a satire upon a public enemy, or as a missionary tract—whose subtle purpose was the reform of morals, the purgation of society, or the destruction of Popery,—and there is none of these preposterous theories which has not been maintained by bearded men, in and out of Spain,—is grievously to misread the book and to mistake the writer. Had it been any of these things, *Don Quixote* would have died when it achieved its purpose. What has made the fortune of the book and endowed it with its singular gift of possessing a charm for humanity for all time to come, as popular out of Spain as among Spaniards, though steeped in the very

essence of *Españolismo*, is that Cervantes had real material
in his own life to furnish his imagination. He drew from
his own experience when he pictured the man full of the
romantic ideal, with a soul thirsting for the redress of
wrongs and fired with visions of the old chivalry, entering upon the field of life in search of adventures. Don
Quixote is but the image of his creator, as his wanderings in quest of wrongs to redress, in imitation of the
ancient knights-errant, are but a pale reflex of the strange
career of trouble, disaster, and humiliation which was
lived by Cervantes himself in the pursuit of honour and
all noble and manly purpose. To that ardent spirit,
entering life with his imagination stored, as we know that
it was, with the images of the old romances, in an age
when his country seemed to be at the head of the world—
himself destined to take a part in a scene which recalled
the glories of the fabled chivalry, when Don John, himself a living embodiment of Amadis and Palmerin, and in
person and character most what the ideal knight-errant
should be, stepped a galliard with his noble captains on
the quarter-deck of the admiral's galley in pure joy of
heart at the advancing host of the Paynim—to the young
Cervantes it might well appear that the old order had
come again. It was only in his old age that he understood that this was but a passing illusion—that the period
was one fatal to romance and to enthusiasm; and of this
sad later conviction the fruit was *Don Quixote.*

He has been ever since the progenitor of a
numerous race, of which Hudibras and Uncle Toby,
Colonel Newcome and Mr. Pickwick, are some of
the members ; but the Knight of La Mancha still over-
tops all his descendants as Amadis overtopped in worth

and valour his children and grandchildren. It is Cervantes' peculiar glory—a glory shared by Shakespeare alone among the sons of men—to have given permanence and immortality to an image of his own making. Nor are his subordinate characters less admirable, both for themselves as living individual creatures, and as accessories in the picture and aids to the development of the fable. Sancho Panza is the perpetual counterfoil of his master—the man of vulgar reason without romance, opposed to the man of fine understanding warped by imagination. These two characters possess the world between them, as Coleridge has said; and it is Cervantes' peculiar happiness that he has been enabled to exhibit them in action, making of the individual creature a permanent type, and so elevating the Manchegan peasant as that he serves, like his master, as the denominator for a whole species. By a subtle stroke of art, which reaches to the profoundest depth of human nature, the victory only remains with the unimaginative, practical man of reason when the enthusiast, the man of intelligence, recovers his wits.

These two, the master and man, have absorbed so much of our interest that the minor characters of the fable, each fitted so perfectly to its part that they seem not to have been specially provided but picked up on the way, have scarcely received their due meed of applause. And yet each has life, as though it lived indeed, and the talk of each is as real and natural as though we had heard it. The Housekeeper and the Niece appear but seldom, and say but a very few words; but we have them moving in the flesh before us—the *ama* with her fussy household loyalty to her master; the *sobrina*—a pert young hussy

who is not afraid to chaff her uncle while in awe of his
humours. Could she have been drawn from Constanza, the
daughter of Andrea, Cervantes' sister, who was a constant
inmate of her uncle's modest home? The Priest, with
his genial tact and keen good sense ; Master Nicholas,
the Barber, a maladroit and blundering vulgar person, are
portraits which might have figured on the canvas of
Velasquez. The various travellers met on the road
—the irascible Biscayan—the pursey silk-merchants
of Toledo—the shrewd and witty Vivaldo—the friars,
the shepherds, the goatherds, the students, with all
the company at the various inns, and at Camacho's
wedding — Ginés de Pasamonte, that pleasant rogue,
and Roque Guinart, the robber of milder mood—Ricote,
the Morisco—Don Diego de Miranda, the superior
country-gentleman, with the rest of the higher quality,
including the somewhat heartless and selfish though
courteous Duke and his laughter-loving Duchess—not to
speak of Samson Carrasco, the student and wit of the
larger intelligence, who plays so important a *rôle* in the
dispelling of Don Quixote's craze ; and the women-
kind, Maritornes the tender-hearted—the too precise
and sententious Marcela—Dorothea, the beautiful and
discreet — Sancho's wife and daughter, with, finally,
Aldonza Lorenzo, that sturdy lass, able, according to
Sancho, to "pitch a bar as well as the stoutest lad in the
parish," who is elected to be Dulcinea—they have all
and each a distinct individuality, being more real than
any creatures of flesh and blood. And then the innkeepers—what varied entertainment do they furnish!
There are five of them, and no two are alike, from the
canting rogue who falls into Don Quixote's humour and

dubs him knight, to Juan Palomeque, the sulky and
left-handed, who has Sancho tossed in the blanket.
By a few touches they come into life; and are not so
much made as creatures always existing, who are casually
met in the process of the story. It is an early plough-
man plodding to the field, chanting as he goes the
ballad of Roncesvalles; or it is the cheery young
soldier, with his bundle slung by his sword on his
shoulder, singing that he is bound to the wars for want
of pence and had he a penny he wouldn't go hence.
Slight as the episode is, and of no apparent connection
with the story, we should have missed it had it not been
there, to give a gleam of light and colour on a scene
which, from its nature, is inclined to be monotonous.
The people talk, not as if they wanted to be reported,
but as they actually did talk and had been overheard.
Other humorists are fain to call attention to the
comedy by making either some of the puppets explain
that they are there to make sport, or by the showman
intruding his person among them, as Master Peter's
boy did, at the famous show of Don Gaiferos and the
Fair Melisendra. But Cervantes is content to let his
creatures talk and act as they list, moved only by internal
impulse. Let us take, as a capital instance of his power,
the scene at Don Quixote's house-door, when Sancho is
trying to push his way in and the niece and housekeeper
are stoutly resisting. The clamour of female tongues is
distinctly heard, and we can see the two women holding
the door against Sancho, who is shouting "Housekeeper
of Satan!" and demanding his governorship. Or let us
intrude upon the circle at the castle where Sancho is
seated with the Duchess and her damsels, who has

I 2

asked him some delicate questions about his master and Dulcinea. Do we not see him, with his finger on his lips, and stealthy steps, as he cautiously feels along the hangings to see if there is any one listening before he answers ?

The medium through which his effects are produced is admirably fitted to Cervantes' purpose. The contrast between the knight's lofty designs and their commonplace or sordid surroundings becomes heightened by the use of a language of inimitable simplicity, clearness, and directness. Cervantes was not one of those who are infected by what Bacon has called that " first distemper of learning, when men study words and not matter." He had no vanity of style, but used language merely to express his thoughts, without caring to attract attention for the children of his wit by their fine clothing. While master of a style of infinite fascination, flexible, graceful, picturesque, fit clothing for every noble thought and human fancy, and able to wield the Castilian so that it became a new power—assuming a nobility of tone and compactness of structure such as it never possessed before or has had since—Cervantes disdains, except with the deliberate intention of ridiculing, the usual tricks and artifices of the "stylist." He is not "precious " of speech. He does not seek to invest common ideas with a false air of price by giving them uncommon expression. Rather it is his uncommon ideas which are heightened by common words. No great writer is perhaps habitually so careless of rhetorical effect as Cervantes, and in none of his works is this carelessness carried so far as in his master-piece. Although abounding in passages of beauty and eloquence, such as exhibit the resources of the Spanish language in their highest perfection, he is the despair of exact critics like Señor Clemencin, his unrelenting and ample commentator. He is better in the Second Part than in the First, which he evidently launched into the current without being quite sure of where it would be carried; but generally the language of *Don Quixote* is, for a classic, loose, irregular, and incorrect. Sometimes a sentence is left in the air, with the predicate wanting. Sometimes the parts do not join, or there is a confusion of relatives, or a discord of antecedents. But never is the writer false, or affected, or vain with the vanity of the pen, except in the way of burlesque, and to suit the character speaking, or the situation.

Such as it is, no great work was ever achieved by the pen which can fairly be set against this book of Cervantes; nor among the great writers who have contributed to the everlasting delight and entertainment of the world is there any with a claim higher upon the gratitude of mankind than he, the story of whose romantic and adventurous life I have endeavoured to tell.

INDEX.

BIBLIOGRAPHY.

BY

JOHN P. ANDERSON

(British Museum).

I. WORKS.

Obras. 16 vols. Madrid, 1803-5, 8vo.

Obras escogidas. Nueva edicion clásica, arreglada, corregida é ilustrada con notas por D. Augustin Garcia de Arrieta. (Vida de M. de Cervantes Saavedra. Por D. Martin Fernandez de Navarrete. Análisis, ó juicio crítico del Quijote. Por D. Augustin Garcia de Arrieta.) 10 tom. Paris, 1827, 16mo.

Obras escogidas. 11 tom. Madrid, 1829, 8vo.

Obras. Segunda edicion. Madrid, 1849, 8vo.
Tom. i. of the "Biblioteca de Autores Españoles," by B. C. Aribau.

Obras Completas de Cervantes. [Edited, with notes, by J. E. Hartzenbusch and C. Rosell.] (Vida de M. de C. S. escrita por B. C. Aribau. Nuevas investigaciones acerca de la vida y obras de Cervantes por C. A. de la Barrera.—Notas a las Nuevas Investigaciones, etc.) 12 tom. Madrid, Argamasilla de Alba, 1863, 1864, 8vo.

II. COLLECTIONS OF WORKS.

La Galatea. Va añadido el Viage del Parnaso, etc. 2 parts. Madrid, 1614, 4to.
La Galatea, dividida en seis libros. Va añadido El Viage del Parnaso. 2 parts. Madrid, 1736, 4to.
——Another edition. Madrid, 1772, 4to.
Viage al Parnaso compuesto por M. de Cervantes. Publicanse ahora de nuevo una tragedia y una comedia ineditas del mismo; aquella intitulada la Numancia, este el Trato de Argel. Madrid, 1784, 8vo.
Galatea, el Viage al Parnaso, y Obras Dramaticas. Nueva edicion. (Por D. M. F. de Navarrete.) Paris, 1841, 8vo.
  Tom. xxv. of the "Coleccion de los mejores autores Españoles."
Varias obras inéditas de Cervantes, sacadas de códices de la Biblioteca Colombina, con nuevas ilustraciones sobre la vida del autor y el Quijote, por A. de Castro. Madrid, 1874, 8vo.
The Voyage to Parnassus; Numantia, a tragedy; the Commerce of Algiers. By Cervantes. Translated from the Spanish by G. W. J. Gyll. London, 1870, 8vo.
  One of A. Murray's Reprints.

III. DRAMATIC WORKS.

Ocho Comedias, y ocho Entremeses nuevos, nunca representados. Madrid, 1615, 4to.
First edition, and very rare.

Comedias y Entremeses; con una dissertacion o prologo sobre las comedias de España. 2 tom. Madrid, 1749, 8vo.
Ocho entremeses de M. de Cervantes Saavedra. Tercera impresion. Cadiz, 1816, 12mo.
Los Entremeses de M. de Cervantes Saavedra. Ilustrados con preciosas viñetas. Madrid, 1868, 8vo.
Comedias y Entremeses. Numancia. La Entretenida. El Juez de los divorcios. El Rufian viudo llmado Trampagos. Eleccion de los Alcaldes de Daganzo. La Guarda Cuidadosa y el Vizcaino Fingido. Precedidas de una introduccion. Madrid, 1875, 4to.
Numantia: a tragedy translated from the Spanish, with introduction and notes, by James Y. Gibson. London, 1885, 8vo.

IV. POEMS.

Cervantes esclavo y cantor del Santísimo Sacremento. (Poesías inéditas de Cervantes.) MS. de la Bib. Floreciana de la Real Academia de la Historia, y artículo del Sr. D. A. Fernandez Guerra y Orbe. De la Revista Agustiniana. Valladolid, 1882, 8vo.

V. DON QUIXOTE—*Spanish.*

El Ingenioso Hidalgo Don Quixote de la Mancha. Compuesto por Miguel de Cervantes Saavedra, etc. Juan de la Cuesta: Madrid, 1605, 4to.
  This is the first edition of Don Quixote. The licence is dated the

26th of September 1604; and the certificate for errata December 1, 1604.

——Second edition. Juan de la Cuesta: Madrid, 1605, 4to.

The Privilege is dated 9th February 1605.

——Another edition. Jorge Rodriguez: Lisboa, 1605, 4to.

"Aprobacion" and licence dated Lisbon, February 26 and March 1, 1605.

——Another edition. P. Crasbeeck: Lisboa, 1605, 8vo.

Licensed March 27 and 29.

——Another edition. P. P. Mey: Valencia, 1605, 8vo.

The "Aprobacion" is dated July 18, 1605. Another edition, according to Salvá y Mallen, was issued from the Mey press in 1605.

——Another edition. R. Vulpius: Brusselas, 1607, 12mo.

——Another edition. Juan de la Cuesta: Madrid, 1608, 4to.

The true second edition; commonly called the third edition.

——Another edition. P. Locarni y J. B. Bidello: Milan, 1610, 8vo.

——Another edition. R. Vulpius y H. Antonio: Brucelas, 1611, 8vo.

——Another edition. Huberto Antonio: Brucelas, 1617, 8vo.

Segunda Parte del Ingenioso Cavallero Don Quixote de la Mancha. Juan de la Cuesta: Madrid, 1615, 4to.

This is the first edition of Cervantes' Second Part.

——Another edition. P. P. Mey: Valencia, 1616, 8vo.

——Another edition. Huberto Antonio: Brucelas, 1616, 8vo.

——Another edition. Jorge Rodriguez: Lisboa, 1617, 4to.

——El Ingenioso Hidalgo Don Quixote de la Mancha. Segunda

parte del Ingenioso Cavallero Don Quixote de la Mancha, etc. Barcelona, 1617, 8vo.

The first complete edition of the two parts, according to Salvá.

——Primera y segunda parte del Ingenioso Hidalgo, etc. 2 vols. Francisco Martinez: Madrid, 1637, 4to.

The first complete edition, according to Navarrete.

——Primera y segunda parte del Ingenioso Hidalgo Don Quixote de la Mancha. En la Imprenta Real: Madrid, 1647, 4to.

A reprint of the preceding.

——Primera y segunda parte, etc. Melchor Sanchez: Madrid, 1655, 4to.

——Parte primera y segunda del ingenioso hidalgo D. Quixote de la Mancha. Madrid, 1662, 4to.

——Vida y hechos del Ingenioso Cavallero Don Quixote de la Mancha. Nueva edicion, coregida y ilustrada con differentes estampas. 2 parts. Bruselas, 1662, 8vo.

First illustrated edition, as also the first in which the title was altered to Vida y Hechos, etc.

——Parte primera y segunda, etc. Madrid, 1668, 4to.

The Second Part bears the date 1662.

——Vida y hechos del ingenioso cavallero, etc. 2 vols. Bruselas, 1671, 8vo.

——Vida y Hechos del ingenioso Cavallero Don Quixote de la Mancha. Nueva edicion, corregida y illustrada con 32 estampas. 2 pts. Amberes, 1673-72, 8vo.

——Another edition. 2 pts. Madrid, 1674, 4to.

——Nueva edicion, corregida y ilustrada con 32 differentes

estampas. 2 pts. Amberes, 1697, 8vo.
——Another edition. 2 vols. Barcelona, 1704, 4to.
——Another edition. 2 tom. Madrid, 1706, 4to.
A reprint of the Madrid edition of 1674.
——Nueva edicion corregida é ilustrada con treinta y cinco laminas, etc. 2 tom. Madrid, 1714, 4to.
——Nueva edicion, etc. 2 pts. Amberes, 1719, 8vo.
——Another edition. 2 pts. Madrid, 1723, 4to.
——Nueva edicion corregida, etc. 2 tom. Madrid, 1730, 4to.
——Another edition. 2 tom. Madrid, 1735, 4to.
——Another edition. 2 tom. Leon de Francia (Lyons), 1736, 8vo.
——Another edition. (Advertencias de J. Oldfield sobre las estampas. Vida de Cervantes Saavedra, autor Don G. Mayans i Siscar.) [Edited by P. Pineda.] 4 tom. Londres, 1738, 4to.
The first critical edition.
——Another edition. 2 tom. Madrid, 1741, 4to.
——Another edition. Con muy bellas estampas. (Vida de M. de Cervantes Saavedra. Autor Don G. Mayans i Siscar.) 4 tom. Haia, 1744, 8vo.
——Nueva edicion, corregida, ilustrada, y añadida con quarenta y quatro laminas, etc. 2 tom. Madrid, 1750, 8vo.
——Another edition. 2 tom. Madrid, 1750, 4to.
——Another edition. 2 tom. Madrid, 1751, 4to.

——Another edition. 4 tom. Amsterdam, 1755, 12mo.
A reprint of the Hague edition.
——Another edition. 4 tom. Barcelona, 1755, 8vo.
——Another edition. 4 tom. Tarragona, 1757, 8vo.
——Nueva edicion, corregida, e ilustrada con quarenta y quatro laminas. (Vida de M. de Cervantes Saavedra. Su autor G. Mayans i Siscar.) 2 tom. Madrid, 1764-65, 4to.
——Another edition. 4 vols. Madrid, 1765, 8vo.
——Another edition. 4 tom. Madrid, 1771, 8vo.
——Nueva edicion, corregida, y ilustrada con várias laminas, y la vida del autor [by G. Mayans y Siscar]. 4 tom. Madrid, 1777, 8vo.
——Nueva edicion, corregida por la Real Academia Española. (Vida de Cervantes y analisis del Quixote [by V. de los Rios].) 4 tom. Madrid, 1780, 4to.
The first critical edition printed in Spain.
——Another edition. Con annotaciones, indices y varias lecciones por el Reverendo J. Bowle. 6 tom. Londres and Salisbury, 1781, 4to.
——Nueva edicion, corregida por la Real Academia Española. (Vida de Cervantes y analysis del Quixote [by V. de los Rios].) 4 tom. Madrid, 1782, 8vo.
Second Academy edition.
——Vida y hechos del Ingenioso Hidalgo, etc. 4 tom. Madrid, 1782, 8vo.
——El Ingenioso Hidalgo Don Quixote de la Mancha. Tercera edicion, corregida por la Real

Academia Española. 6 tom. Madrid, 1787, 8vo.
——Another edition. 6 tom. Madrid, 1797-98, 16mo.
——Nueva edicion, corregida de-nuevo; con nuevas notas, con nuevas estampas, con nuevo analisis, y con la vida de el autor nuevamente aumentada por J. A. Pellicer. 7 tom. in 6. Madrid, 1797-98, 8vo.
Six copies of this edition were printed on vellum.
——Another edition. Corregido de nuevo, con nuevas notas, con nuevas viñetas por J. A. Pellicer. 9 tom. Madrid, 1798-1800, 12mo.
——Another edition. 6 vols. Leipzig, 1800, 12mo.
——Another edition. 4 tom. Burdeos, 1804, 12mo.
——Vida y hechos del Ingenioso e caballero D. Quijote de la Mancha. 6 tom. Madrid, 1804, 8vo.
——Another edition. (Vida de M. de Cervantes Saavedra escrita por D. J. A. Pellicer.—Notas.) [Edited by C. L. Ideler.] 6 tom. Berlin, 1804-5, 8vo.
——El Ingenioso hidalgo D. Quijote de la Mancha. 4 tom. Londres, 1808, 18mo.
——Another edition. Historia del ingenioso hidalgo Don Quixote de la Mancha. 6 tom. Barcelona, 1808-14, 12mo.
——Another edition. Vida y hechos, etc. 4 vols. Madrid, 1808, 8vo.
——Another edition. El Ingenioso Hidalgo, etc. 4 vols. Lyons, 1810, 12mo.
——Another edition. 6 vols. Paris, 1814, 8vo.

——Another edition. El Ingenioso Hidalgo Don Quixote de la Mancha. Nueva edicion corregida por F. Fernandez. 4 tom. London, 1814, 12mo.
A reprint of the 1808 edition.
——Another edition. 4 tom. Burdeos, 1815, 12mo.
——El Ingenioso Hidalgo, etc. 6 vols. Leipzig, 1818, 8vo.
A reprint of the Leipzig edition of 1800.
——Cuarta edicion corregida por la Real Academia Española. (Con vida por Navarrete.) 5 tom. Madrid, 1819, 8vo.
——Another edition. 4 vols. Paris, 1825, 12mo.
——Another edition. 2 vols. Madrid, 1826, 12mo.
——Edicion en miniatura enter-amente conforme à la ultima corregida y publicada por la Real Academia Española. [Edited by J. M. de Ferrer.] Paris, 1827, 12mo.
——Another edition. 6 vols. Paris, 1827, 12mo.
——Another edition. 2 tom. Zaragoza, 1831, 8vo.
——Another edition. 4 vols. Madrid, 1831, 16mo.
——Another edition. 4 vols. Barcelona, 1832, 8vo.
A reprint of the Academy edition of 1819.
——Another edition. Paris, 1832, 32mo.
——Another edition. Comentado por D. Clemencin. 6 tom. Madrid, 1833-39, 4to.
——Another edition. Con el elogio de Cervantes por D. J. Mor de Fuentes. Paris, 1835, 8vo.
Tom. i. of the "Coleccion de los mejores Autores Españoles."

Don Quixote. Another edition. Boston, 1836, 8vo.
A third edition appeared in 1842.
——Another edition. 4 vols. Paris, 1838, 16mo.
——Another edition. Con la vida de Cervantes por M. F. de Navarrete. Paris, 1840, 8vo.
Tom. i. of the "Coleccion de los mejores Autores Españoles."
——Edicion adornada con laminas. Segunda edicion. 2 tom. Barcelona, 1840, 4to.
——Another edition. 2 vols. Mexico, 1842, 8vo.
——Another edition. 2 vols. Barcelona, 1848, 8vo.
——Novisima edicion clásica, ilustrada con notas historicas gramaticales y criticas, segun las de la Academia Española y sus individuos de numero Pellicer, Arrieta, Clemencin, y por F. Sales. Aumentada con el Buscapié, anotado por A. de Castro. (Apendice contiene observaciones criticas [by J. E. Hartzenbusch]. Vida de M. de Cervantes.) Madrid, 1850, 8vo.
——Another edition. 2 vols. Paris, 1850, 8vo.
——Another edition. New York, 1853, 12mo.
——Another edition. Paris, 1855, 8vo.
——Another edition. Don Quijote de la Mancha. Nueva edicion. Ilustrada, etc. 2 tom. Madrid, 1855-56, 8vo.
——Another edition. Madrid, 1855, 8vo.
——El Ingenioso Hidalgo Don Quijote de la Mancha. [Illustrated edition.] 2 pts. Barcelona, 1859, fol.

——Another edition. 3 vols. Madrid, 1862-63, fol.
——Edicion corregida con especial estudio de la primera, por D. J. E. Hartzenbusch. 4 tom. Argamasilla de Alba, 1863, 8vo.
——Novisima edicion, con notas historicas de la Academia Española, Pellicer, Arrieta. Aumentada del Buscapié, anotado por A. de Castro. Adornado con 300 grabados y el retrato del autor. Madrid, 1865, 8vo.
——Another edition. 2 pts. Leipzig, 1866, 8vo.
Tom. iii., iv. of the "Coleccion de Autores Españoles."
——Another edition. Tom. 1. Madrid, 1868, 8vo.
No more published.
——La primera edicion del Ingenioso Hidalgo Don Quijote de la Mancha, reproducida en facsímile por la foto-tipografía, y publicada por F. Lopez Fábra. [With notes by J. E. Hartzenbusch.] 2 pts. Barcelona, 1871-74, 4to.
——Edicion conforme á la última corregida por la Academia Española, con notas, etc. Paris, 1873, 8vo.
——Vida de M. de Cervantes por R. Leon Mainez. (El Ingenioso Hidalgo Don Quijote de la Mancha publicado bajo la direccion de R. Leon Mainez.) Tom. 1-5. Cádiz, 1876-77, etc., 8vo.
——El Ingenioso Hidalgo Don Quijote de la Mancha. Sevilla, 1879, 16mo.
——Another edition. 2 tom. Madrid, 1880, 16mo.

Don Quixote. Nueva edicion, con notas sobre el texto, del puño y letra del autor, en el ejemplar prueba de correccion de la 1ª edicion de 1605, etc. [Edited by F. Ortego Aguirrebeña.] 2 tom. Palencia, 1884(-83), 8vo.

An impudent forgery.

——Novísima edición aumentado con El Buscapié. Adornado con grabados. Madrid, 1887, 8vo.

DON QUIXOTE—*English.*

Shelton's Translation—
The History of Don Quichote. [Translated from the Spanish by T. Shelton.] 2 pts. G. Blounte: London, 1620, 4to.

Part i. has no title-page. The date 1620 appears on the title-page of Part ii. Mr. Watts has discovered that the first edition has a title-page to Part i. with the date 1612, and he says he only knows of one existing copy.

——Another edition. London, 1652, fol.

——Another edition. London, 1675, fol.

——Another edition. The History of the most Ingenious Knight Don Quixote de la Mancha. Formerly made English by T. Shelton: now revised and partly new translated by J. Stevens. Second edition. 2 vols. London, 1706, 8vo.

——Another edition. Translated into English by T. Shelton, and now printed verbatim from the 4to edition of 1620. With cuts from the French of Coypel. 4 vols. London, 1725, 12mo.

Philips's Translation—
The History of Don Quixote of

Mancha: and his trusty Squire Sancho Pancha. Now made English, and adorned with several copper plates. By J. P(hilips). London, 1687, fol.

Motteux's Translation—
The History of the renowned Don Quixote. Translated by several hands, and publish'd by P. Motteux. 4 vols. London, 1701, 12mo.

——The History of the renowned Don Quixote. Translated by several hands, and publish'd by P. Motteux. Adorn'd with sculptures. The third edition. 4 vols. London, 1712, 12mo.

——Fourth edition, revised by J. Ozell. 4 vols. London, 1719, 12mo.

——Fifth edition. 4 vols. London, 1725, 12mo.

——Another edition, revised anew by Mr. Ozell. With explanatory notes. 4 vols. Edinburgh, 1766, 12mo.

——Another edition. 4 vols. Edinburgh, 1803, 12mo.

——Another edition. The History of the Ingenious Gentleman Don Quixote de la Mancha. A new edition, with copious notes; and an essay on the life and writings of Cervantes [by J. G. Lockhart]. 5 vols. Edinburgh, 1822, 8vo.

——Another edition. The History of Don Quixote de la Mancha. A new edition, divested of cumbrous matter and revised for general reading. To which is prefixed a sketch of the life and writings of the author. London, 1847, 12mo.

——Another edition. Adventures of Don Quixote de la Mancha.

I 3

New and revised edition. London [1877], 8vo.
Part of the "Chandos Classics."
——Another edition. The History of the Ingenious Gentleman Don Quixote of la Mancha, etc. [With a life of the author, and notes by J. G. Lockhart, and with etchings by A. Lalauze.] 4 vols. Edinburgh, 1879-84, 8vo.
——Another edition. The History of Don Quixote of la Mancha. Edited, with notes and memoir, by J. G. Lockhart, preceded by a short notice of Motteux, by H. Van Laun. With etchings by R. de los Rios. 4 vols. London, 1880-81, 8vo.
——Another edition. The Achievements of the Ingenious Gentleman Don Quixote de la Mancha. A translation based on that of P. A. Motteux, with the memoir and notes of J. G. Lockhart. Edited by E. Bell. 2 vols. London, 1882, 8vo.
Part of "Bohn's Standard Library."
Ward's Translation—
The Life and Adventures of Don Quixote translated into Hudibrastick Verse, by E. Ward. 2 vols. London, 1711-12, 8vo.
Jarvis's Translation—
The Life and Exploits of the Ingenious Gentleman, Don Quixote of La Mancha. Translated by Charles Jarvis. 2 vols. London, 1742, 4to.
——Second edition. 2 vols. London, 1749, 8vo.
——Third edition. 2 vols. London, 1756, 4to.
——Another edition. Now carefully revised and corrected;

with a new translation of the Spanish Poetry: to which is prefixed a new life of Cervantes; including a critique on the Quixote: also a chronological plan of the work; embellished with new engravings, and a map of Spain. 4 vols. London, 1801, 8vo.
——Another edition. 4 vols. London, 1809, 16mo.
——Another edition. With engravings. 4 vols. London, 1819, 8vo.
——Another edition. The Life and Adventures of Don Quixote de la Mancha. A new edition, with engravings from designs by R. Westall. 4 vols. London, 1820, 8vo.
——Another edition. The Life and Exploits of Don Quixote de la Mancha. 4 vols. London, 1821, 12mo.
——Another edition. The Life and Exploits of Don Quixote de la Mancha. Translated by C. Jarvis. (Illustrated by 24 designs by Cruickshank.) 2 vols. London, 1831, 12mo.
——Another edition. Carefully revised and corrected. Illustrated by Tony Johannot. 3 vols. London, 1837-39, 8vo.
——Another edition. Adventures of Don Quixote de la Mancha. Carefully revised and corrected. Illustrated by Tony Johannot. 2 vols. London [1852], 8vo.
——Another edition. London, 1856, 8vo.
——Another edition. The History of Don Quixote. (The English text is that of Jarvis, with occasional corrections from Motteux's translations.) The

text edited by J. W. Clark, and a biographical notice of Cervantes, by T. T. Shore. Illustrated by G. Doré. London [1864-67], 4to.

——Another edition. The Adventures of Don Quixote de la Mancha. With a memoir of the author. Illustrated by Tony Johannot. 10 pts. London [1864-65], 8vo.
No more published.

——Another edition. With illustrations. London, 1866 [1865], 8vo.

——Another edition. With illustrations by A. B. Houghton, engraved by the Brothers Dalziel. London, 1866, 8vo.

——Another edition. Carefully revised and corrected. Illustrated by Tony Johannot. London [1870], 8vo.
Part of "Beeton's Boy's Own Library."

——Another edition. London [1870-72], 4to.
Re-issued in 1876-78.

——Another edition. Illustrated by Tony Johannot. London [1879], 8vo.

——Another edition. London [1880], 4to.

——Another edition. London [1881], 8vo.
Part of the "Excelsior Series."

——People's edition. 2 pts. London [1882], 4to.

——Another edition. El Ingenioso Hidalgo Don Quixote de la Mancha. With an introduction by H. Morley. 2 vols. London, 1885, 8vo.
Vol. xxv. of "Morley's Universal Library."

——Another edition. El Ingenioso Hidalgo Don Quixote de

la Mancha. Translated by C. Jarvis. With an introduction by H. Morley. 2 pts. London, 1890 [1889], 8vo.
Part of "Routledge's Popular Library." A stereotyped reprint of the edition published in "Morley's Universal Library" in 1885.

Smollett's Translation—
The History and Adventures of Don Quixote. To which is prefixed some account of the author's life. By T. Smollett. Illustrated with twenty-eight new copperplates designed by Hayman, etc. 2 vols. London, 1755, 4to.

——Second edition. 4 vols. London, 1761, 8vo.

——Another edition. 4 vols. London, 1782, 8vo.

——Fifth edition, corrected. 4 vols. London, 1782, 12mo.

——Sixth edition. 4 vols. London, 1792, 12mo.

——Sixth edition. 4 vols. London, 1793, 12mo.

——Another edition. 4 vols. Dublin, 1796, 8vo.

——Cooke's edition. 5 vols. London [1799], 12mo.

Miscellaneous Translations—
The delightful history of Don Quixot. Also the Comical Humours of his facetious Squire Sancho Panza, etc. [An abridged translation by E. S.] London, 1689, 12mo.

——The history of the renowned Don Quixote de la Mancha. Translated into English by G. Kelly, Esq. To which are added notes, with copperplates. 4 vols. London, 1769, 12mo.

——Don Quixote de la Mancha. Translated from the Spanish [by M. Smirke]. Embellished with engravings from pictures painted by R. Smirke, Esq., R. A. 4 vols. London, 1818, 4to.

——Don Quixote de la Mancha. Translated from the Spanish [or rather compiled for the most part from previous translations. With plates.] London, 1877, 8vo.

——The Ingenious Knight, Don Quixote de la Mancha. A new translation from the originals of 1605 and 1608, by A. J. Duffield, with some of the notes of J. Bowle, J. A. Pellicer, D. Clemencin, and other commentators. 3 vols. London, 1881 [1880], 8vo.

——Don Quixote, from the Spanish, with 30 Illustrations by Sir John Gilbert, Tony Johannot, and others. London, 1882, 8vo.
Part of "Routledge's Sixpenny Series."

——The Ingenious Gentleman, Don Quixote of la Mancha. A translation, with introduction and notes, by John Ormsby. 4 vols. London, 1885, 8vo.

——The Ingenious Gentleman, Don Quixote of La Mancha. A new edition; done into English, with notes, original and selected, and a new life of the author. By H. E. Watts. 5 vols. London, 1888, 4to.

DON QUIXOTE—*Abridgments.*

El Quijote de los Niños y para el Pueblo. Abreviado por un entusiasta de su Autor. Madrid, 1856, 16mo.

El Quijote para Todos, abreviado y anotado por un Entusiasta de su Autor. Madrid, 1856, 8vo.

The much esteemed History of Don Quixote de la Mancha (contracted from the original). London, 1699, 12mo.

The History of the ever-renowned Knight Don Quixote, etc. [Abridged from the work of Cervantes.] London [1700 ?], 4to.
A Chap-book.

The much-esteemed History of Don Quixote de la Mancha, etc. 2 pts. London, 1716, 12mo.

The most admirable and delightful History of the atchievements of Don Quixote de la Mancha, etc. London, 1721, 12mo.

The life and exploits of Don Quixote de la Mancha abridged. London, 1778, 12mo.

The history of Don Quixote; with an account of his exploits. Abridged [from Smollett's translation]. Halifax, 1839, 16mo.

The Story of Don Quixote and his Squire Sancho Panza. By M. Jones. [With illustrations.] London, 1871, 8vo.

The Wonderful Adventures of Don Quixote de la Mancha. Abridged and adapted to youthful capacities by Sir Marvellous Crackjoke. With illustrations by K. Meadows and J. Gilbert. London [1872], 4to.

The Adventures of Don Quixote adapted for young readers, and illustrated with coloured pictures. London [1883], 4to.

DON QUIXOTE—*Extracts.*

Manuel Alfabético de Quijote, ó coleccion de pensamientos de Cervantes en su immortal obra, ordenados con algunas notas por Dou [Mariano] de R[ementeria?]. Madrid, 1838, 16mo. Sentencias de Don Quijote y Agudezas de Sancho. Máximas y pensamientos mas notables contenidos en la obra de Cervantes, Don Quijote de la Mancha. Madrid, 1863, 16mo.

Cervantes as a novelist; from a selection of the episodes and incidents of the popular romance of Don Quixote. [With coloured plates.] London, 1822, 8vo.

Stories and chapters from Don Quixote versified. London [1830], 12mo.

Sancho Panza's Proverbs, and others which occur in Don Quixote; with a literal English translation, notes, and an introduction by U. R. Burke. London, 1872, 8vo.
  Only 36 copies privately printed.
——Another edition. Spanish Salt, a collection of all the proverbs which are to be found in Don Quixote. London, 1877, 8vo.

Wit and Wisdom of Don Quixote. New York, 1867, 12mo.
——Another edition. With a biographical sketch of Cervantes, by Emma Thompson. Boston, 1882, 8vo.

The Adventures of Don Quixote. (A selection. The engravings are borrowed from the edition illustrated by Gustave Doré.) London, 1885, 8vo.

The poetry of the "Don Quixote" of Don Miguel de Cervantes Saavedra done into English by J[ames] Y[oung] G[ibson], Scotus. (In vol. 2 of "The Cid Ballads," by J. Y. Gibson, London, 1887.)

DON QUIXOTE—*Appendix.*

Aguilar, P. de.—Memorias del Cautivo en la Goleta de Túnez, el Alférez P. de Aguilar [mentioned by Cervantes in chaps. 39-41 of Part I. of Don Quixote]. Madrid, 1875, 8vo.
  Published by the "Sociedad de Bibliófilos Españolas."

Ahmad Benengeli.—Adiciones á la Historia del Ingenioso Hidalgo Don Quixote de la Mancha. Madrid [1770?], 8vo.

Alcides.—El Alcides de la Mancha, el famoso Don Quixote. De un ingenio de esta corte. Comedia. Madrid, 1750, 4to.

Almar, George.—Don Quixote; or, the Knight of the Woeful Countenance. A musical drama, in two acts. London [1833?], 12mo.
  In vol. xiv. of "Cumberland's Minor Theatre."

Antequera, Ramon. — Juicio Analítico del Quijote, escrito en Argamasilla de Alba. Madrid, 1863, 8vo.

Anzarena, C. de.—Vida y empressas literarias del ingeniosissimo caballero Don Quixote de la Manchuela. Parte primera. Sevilla [1767], 8vo.
  No more published.

Armengol, A. C.—El " Quijote " en Boston. Madrid, 1874, 8vo.

Baretti, Joseph. — Tolondron. Speeches to John Bowle about his edition of Don Quixote, etc. London, 1786, 8vo.

Beneke, Juan Basilico. — Colleccion de vocablos, y frases dificiles que occurren en Don Quixote de la Mancha, etc. Leipsique, 1808, 16mo.

Biedermann, F. B. F. — Don Quichotte, et la tâche de ses traducteurs, etc. Paris, 1837, 8vo.

Bowle, John.—A Letter to the Rev. Dr. Percy, concerning a new and classical edition of Don Quixote de la Mancha, etc. London, 1777, 8vo.

Caballero, F. A.—Pericia geografica de Miguel de Cervantes, demostrada con la historia de Don Quijote de la Mancha. Madrid, 1840, 8vo.

Calderon, Juan.—Cervantes vindicado en ciento y quince pasajes del texto del Ingenioso Hidalgo D. Quijote de la Mancha. Madrid, 1854, 8vo.

Cervantes, Miguel de. — Don Quixote de la Manche; Comedie (founded on the work of Cervantes). Paris, 1640, 4to.

——Der Spannische Waghalss: oder des vom Lieb bezauberten Ritters Don Quixote von Quixada gantz neue Auschweifung, etc. [A spurious continuation of Don Quixote.] Nürnberg, 1696, 8vo.

——Les principales avantures de Don Quichotte, representées en figures par Coypel, Picart et antres habiles Maîtres; avec les explications des xxxi. planches tirées de l'original Espagnol. à la Haie, 1746, 4to.

——[The principal adventures of Don Quixote engraved after designs by C. A. Coypel.] London [1775?], obl. 4to.

These engravings are copies on a larger scale of the plates in the preceding work. There are some engravings here not contained in the preceding work, and *vice versâ.*

——Remarks on the proposals lately published [by T. Smollett] for a new translation of Don Quixote, in which will be considered the design of Cervantes in writing the original, and some new lights given relative to his life and adventures. In a letter from a gentleman in the country [*i.e.*, Col. W. Windham]. London, 1755, 8vo.

——Remarks on the extraordinary conduct of the Knight of the Ten Stars, and his Italian Esquire, to the Editor of Don Quixote. In a letter to the Rev. J. S., D.D. London, 1785, 8vo.

A vindication by the Rev. J. Bowle of his edition of *Don Quixote* against Baretti.

——Instrucciones económicas y politicas dadas por el famoso Sancho Panza, gobernador de la insula Bataria, á un hijo suyo. Madrid, 1791, 8vo.

——Historia del mas famoso escudero Sancho Panza desde la gloriosa muerte de Don Quixote de la Mancha, etc. [A continuation of the Don Quixote.] 2 parts. Madrid, 1793-98, 8vo.

——El Buscapié. Opúsculo inédito, que en defensa de la primera parte del Quijote escribió M. de Cervantes Saavedra [!]. Con notas históricas, críticas, i bibliográficas por A. de Castro. Cadiz, 1848, 12mo.

——El Buscapie. With the illustrative notes of A. de Castro. Translated from the Spanish. With a life of the author and some account of his works, by Thomasina Ross. London, 1849, 12mo.

——The "Squib" or Searchfoot, an unedited little work which M. de Cervantes Saavedra wrote in defence of the First Part of the Quijote [?]. Published by A. de Castro, 1847. Translated by a member of the University of Cambridge. Cambridge, 1849, 16mo.

——A los Profanadores del ingenioso hidalgo Don Quijote de la Mancha. Critica y algo mas, por el Diablo con anti-parras. Madrid, 1561, 16mo.

——Iconografía de Don Quijote. Reproduccion heliográfica y foto-tipográfica de 100 láminas elegidas entre las 60 ediciones, diversamente ilustradas, que se han publicado durante 257 años en Barcelona, Paris, Venecia destinadas á la primera edicion de Don Quijote reproducida por lo foto-tipografía por F. Lopez Fábra. Barcelona, 1879, 4to.

Clemencín, Diego.—Indice de las notas de D. Diego Clemencín en su edición de él Ingenioso Hidalgo Don Quijote de la Mancha. Por Carlos F. Brad-ford. Madrid, 1885, 8vo.

Coleridge, Samuel T. — The Literary Remains of Samuel Taylor Coleridge. 4 vols. London, 1836-39, 8vo.
Don Quixote, vol. i., pp. 113-131.

Coll y Vehí, José.—Los Refranes del Quijote ordenados por materias y glosados. Barcelona, 1874, 8vo.

Dawson, George. — Shakespeare and other lectures, etc. London, 1888, 8vo.
Don Quixote, pp. 128-133.

Delgado, J. M.—Adiciones á la historia del ingenioso hidalgo

Don Quixote de la Mancha. Madrid [1770 ?], 8vo.

Diaz de Benjumea, U. — La Estafeta de Urganda : ó aviso sobre el desencanto del Quijote. Londres, 1861, 8vo.

——El Correo de Alquife, ó segundo aviso sobre el desen-canto del Quijote. Barcelona, 1866, 8vo.

——El Mensage de Merlin, ó tercer aviso sobre el desencauto del Quijote. Londres, 1875, 8vo.

——La Verdad sobre el Quijote. Madrid, 1878, 8vo.

Droap, M., *pseud.* — Epístolas Droapianas. Siete cantas sobre Cervantes y el Quixote. Cadiz, 1868, 8vo.

Duffield, A. J.—Don Quixote, his critics and his commentators. With a brief account of the minor works of Cervantes. London, 1881, 8vo.

Dunlop, J. C.—History of Prose Fiction. A new edition. 2 vols. London, 1888, 8vo.
Don Quixote, vol. ii., pp. 313-323.

D'Urfey, Thomas.—The Comical History of Don Quixote. Part I. London, 1694, 4to.

——Part the Second. London, 1694, 4to.

——The Third Part. London, 1696, 4to.

E. T.—Observaciones sobre algunos puntos de la obra de Don Quixote. [Londres, 1807] 8vo.

Eximeno, A.—Apología de Miguel de Cervantes sobre los yerros que se la han notado en el Quixote. Madrid, 1806, 4to.

Fernandez de Avellaneda, A., *pseud.*—Segundo tomo del In-genioso Hidalgo Don Quixote de la Mancha que contieue su tercera salida ; y es la quinta parte de sus aventuras, compuesto por el licenciado A. F. de Avellaneda. Tarragona, 1614, 8vo.

——Vida y Hechos del Ingenioso Hidalgo Don Quixote de la Mancha, etc. Nuevamente añadido por J. Perales y Torres. Madrid, 1732, 4to.

——Nueva edicion. 2 tom. Madrid, 1805, 8vo.

——Another edition. Madrid, 1851, 8vo.

Tom. xviii. of Aribau's " Biblioteca de Autores Españoles."

——A Continuation of the Comical History of the most Ingenious Knight, Don Quixote de la Mancha. By A. F. de Avellaneda. Being a third volume. Translated [from the French version of A. R. le Sage] by J. Stevens. London, 1705, 8vo.

——The History of the Life and Adventures of Don Quixote de la Mancha continued. Now first translated from the original Spanish by Mr. Baker. With cuts. 2 vols. London, 1745, 12mo.

——A Continuation of the History and Adventures of Don Quixote de la Mancha. Translated into English [from the French version of A. R. le Sage] by W. A. Yardley. 2 vols. London, 1784, 8vo.

——The Life and Exploits of Don Quixote de la Mancha, containing his fourth sally, and the fifth part of his adventures written by the licentiate A. F. de Avellaneda, with illustrations and corrections by Don I. Perales y Torres. And now first

translated from the Spanish. Swaffham, 1805, 8vo.

Gayton, Edmund.—Pleasant Notes upon Don Quixot. London, 1654, fol.

——Festivous Notes on the history and adventures of the renowned Don Quixote. London, 1768, 12mo.

Hernandez, Morejon A.—Historia Bibliográfica de la Medecina Española, etc. 7 tom. Madrid, 1842-52, 8vo.

Bellezas de Medicina práctica descubiertas en la obra de Cervantes, tom. ii., pp. 166-180.

——Étude médico-psychologique sur l'histoire de Don Quichotte. Paris, 1858, 8vo.

Inglis, Henry D.—Rambles in the Footsteps of Don Quixote. With illustrations by George Cruickshank. London, 1837, 12mo.

Michaëlis, C. T.—Lessings Minna von Barnhelm und Cervantes' Don Quijote. Berlin, 1883, 8vo.

Montégut, Émile.—Types Littéraires et Fantaises Esthétiques. Paris, 1882, 8vo.

Don Quichotte, pp. 43-92.

Noriéga, F. de Paule.—Critique et defense de Don Quichotte, suivies de chapitres choisies de l'ingenieux Hidalgo, etc. Paris, 1846, 18mo.

Pardo de Figueroa, M.—Droapiana del año 1869. Octava carta sobre Cervantes y el Quijote. Madrid, 1839, 8vo.

Pellícer, J. A.—Exámen crítico del tomo primero de el Anti-Quixote por Nicolas Perez. Madrid, 1806, 12mo.

Perez, N.—El Anti-Quixote. Tom. 1. Madrid, 1805, 8vo.

No more published.

Piernas y Hurtado, José M.—Ideas y noticias del Quijote. Estudio de la obra de Cervantes. Madrid, 1874, 8vo.

Piguenit, D. J.—Don Quixote, an entertainment for music. [By D. J. Piguenit.] London, 1774, 8vo.

——Another edition. London, 1776, 8vo.

Pinelli, B.—Le azioni più celebrate del famoso cavaliere errante Don Chisciotto della Mancha, inventate ed incise da B. Pinelli. Roma [1834 ?] obl. fol.

Pi y Molist, E.—Primores del Don Quijote, en el concepto médico-psicológico, etc. Barcelona, 1886, 8vo.

Sainte-Beuve, C. A.—Nouveaux Lundis. Paris, 1867, 12mo.
   Don Quichotte, tom. viii., pp. 1-65.

Saint-Victor, Paul de.—Hommes et Dieux. Études, etc. Paris, 1867, 8vo.
   Don Quichotte, pp. 411-456.

Salvá, V.—Ha sido juzgado el D. Quijote segun esta obra merece? Paris, 1840, 8vo.

Sbarbi, José María.—Intraducibilidad del Quijote, pasatiempo literario, etc. Madrid, 1876, 8vo.
   Tom. vi. of " El Refranero General Español."

Scherer, Edmond. — Études critiques de Littérature. Paris, 1876, 8vo.
   Don Quichotte, tom. vii., pp. 81-97.

Siñerez, J. F. — El Quijote del siglo xviii. 4 tom. Madrid, 1836, 8vo.

Tubino, Francisco M.—El Quijote y La Estafeta de Urganda [de Nicolas Diaz de Benjumea]. Sevilla, 1862, 8vo.

——Cervantes y el Quijote, Estudios Criticos. Madrid, 1872, 8vo.

Valera, Juan.—Sobre el Quijote y sobre las diferentes maneras de comentarlo y juzgarle. Madrid, 1864, 8vo.

Vidart, Luis. — El Quijote y la clasificacion de las obras literarias, etc. Madrid, 1882, 8vo.

——Los Biógrafos de Cervantes en el siglo xviii., etc. Madrid, 1886, 8vo.

Wildgoose, Geoffrey.—The Spiritual Quixote; or, the summer's ramble of Mr. Geoffrey Wildgoose. A comic romance. [By R. Graves.] 3 vols. London, 1773, 12mo.

——Another edition. 2 vols. Dublin, 1774, 12mo.

Y. T.—Don Quijote de la Mancha en el siglo xix. Cadiz, 1861, 8vo.

VI. GALATEA.

Primera parte de la Galatea, dividida en seys libros. Juan Gracian : Alcala, 1585, 8vo.
   Extremely rare; only one copy known.

——Another edition. Gilles Robinot : Paris, 1611, 8vo.

——Primera parte de la Galatea, dividida en seys libros. Valladolid, 1617, 8vo.

——Los seys libros de la Galatea. Barcelona, 1618, 8vo.

——Another edition. Corregida e ilustrada con laminas finas. 2 tom. Madrid, 1784, 8vo.

——Another edition. 3 vols. Madrid, 1805, 8vo.

——Another edition. 3 vols. Madrid, 1805, 8vo.

——Los seis libros de la Galatea. (Edicion diamante.) Madrid, 1883, 12mo.

——Galatea. A pastoral romance, literally translated from the Spanish by G. W. J. Gyll. London, 1867, 8vo.

VII. NOVELAS—*Spanish.*

Novelas exemplares. J. de la Cuesta: Madrid, 1613, 4to.

First edition. Salvá in his catalogue says this edition is very scarce.

——Second edition. J. de Cuesta: Madrid, 1614, 4to.

Salvá says this edition is even rarer than the first.

——Third edition. N. de Assiayn: Pamplona, 1614, 8vo.

——Fourth edition. R. Velpio y H. Antonio. Brusselas, 1614, 8vo.

——Another edition. N. de Assiayn. Pamplona, 1615, 8vo.

——Another edition. J. B. Bidelo. Milan, 1615, 24mo.

——Another edition. Veneccia, 1616, 12mo.

——Another edition. Lisboa, 1617, 4to.

——Another edition. Pamplona, 1617, 8vo.

——Another edition. Madrid, 1622, 8vo.

——Another edition. Sevilla, 1624, 8vo.

——Another edition. Brusselas, 1625, 8vo.

——Another edition. Barcelona, 1631, 8vo.

——Another edition. Sevilla, 1648, 8vo.

——Another edition. Madrid, 1655, 8vo.

——Another edition. Madrid, 1664, 4to.

——Another edition. Sevilla, 1664, 4to.

——Another edition. Madrid, 1722, 4to.

——Another edition. Barcelona, 1722, 4to.

——Another edition. Añadido un índice de libros de novelas, patrañas, cuentos, hecho por un curioso. Madrid, 1732, 4to.

——Ultima impression. Adornadas de muy bellas estampas. [Edited by P. Pineda.] 2 tom. Haya, 1739, 8vo.

——Nueva impression corregida y adornada con laminas. 2 tom. Madrid, 1783, 8vo.

——Another edition. 2 vols. Valencia, 1797, 8vo.

——Another edition. 3 tom. Madrid, 1799, 12mo.

——Another edition. 3 vols. Madrid, 1803, 8vo.

——Nueva impression corregida y adornada con laminas. 2 tom. Perpiñan, 1816, 12mo.

——Another edition. 2 vols. Madrid, 1821, 8vo.

——Nueva impression, etc. 2 vols. Paris, 1825, 12mo.

——Cervantes Novelas Ejemplares. Mit kritischen und grammatischen Anmerkungen, nebst einem Wörterbuche von P. A. F. Possart. Leipzig, 1833, 8vo.

——Nueva edicion. Paris, 1835, 8vo.

Tom. ii. of the "Coleccion de los mejores Autores Españoles."

——Another edition. 2 vols. Barcelona, 1844, 8vo.

——Another edition. Madrid, 1881, 16mo.

Novelas exemplares. Rinconete y Cortadillo. Edicion ilustrada, etc. Madrid, 1846, 8vo.

—— ——Novelas Ejemplares. (Rinconete y Cortadillo. El Celoso Extremeño. Las Dos Doncellas.) Madrid, 1873, 16mo.

Tom. ix. of the "Biblioteca Universal."

Novelas—*English.*

Exemplarie Novells; in sixe books. The Two Damosels. The Ladie Cornelia. The Liberall Lover. The Force of Bloud. The Spanish Ladie. The Jealous Husband. Turned into English by Don Diego Puede—Ser [*i.e.*, James Mabbe]. London, 1640, fol.

A collection of select novels, written originally in Castillian by Don Miguel Cervantes Saavedra. Made English by H. Bridges. Bristol, 1728, 8vo.

Instructive and entertaining novels. Translated from the original Spanish by T. Shelton. With an account of the work, by a gentleman of the Inner Temple. London, 1742, 12mo. ——Another edition. Dublin, 1747, 12mo.

The Exemplary Novels of M. de Cervantes Saavedra. 2 vols. London, 1822, 12mo.

The Exemplary Novels of M. de Cervantes Saavedra, to which are added El Buscapie, or the Serpent ; and La Tia Fingida, or the Pretended Aunt. Translated by W. K. Kelly. London, 1855, 8vo.

Bohn's Extra Volume Series.

The Exemplary Novels of Miguel de Cervantes Saavedra. Translated by W. K. Kelly. London, 1881, 8vo.

Part of "Bohn's Standard Library."

El Zeloso Estremeno : the Jealous Estremaduran ; a novel done from the Spanish by J. Ozell. London [1710 ?], 8vo.

A dialogue between Scipio and Bergansa, two dogs belonging to Toledo. To which is annexed the history of Rincon and Cortado. Now first translated from the Spanish. London, 1767, 12mo.

The Force of Blood. A novel. Translated from the Spanish of M. de Cervantes Saavedra. London, 1800, 12mo.

Rinconete and Cortadillo.—The Pretended Aunt.—El Amante Liberal. [Translated from the Spanish.] London, 1832, 8vo.

Part of Roscoe's "Spanish Novelists."

VIII. TRABAJOS DE PER-SILES Y SIGISMUNDA.

Los Trabajos de Persiles y Sigismunda, historia setentrional. J. de la Cuesta : Madrid, 1617, 4to.

——Another edition. J. de la Cuesta : Madrid, 1617, 8vo.

——Another edition. N. de Assiayn : Pamplona, 1617, 8vo.

——Another edition. Estevan Richer : Paris, 1617, 8vo.

——Another edition. B. Sorita : Barcelona, 1617, 8vo.

——Another edition. P. P. Mey : Valencia, 1617, 8vo.

——Another edition. Los traba-

jos de Persiles y Sigismunda, historia septentrional. Madrid, 1617 [1750 ?], 4to. A counterfeit reprint.
——Another edition. Brucclas, 1618, 8vo.
——Another edition. Historia de los trabajos de Persiles y Sigismunda corregida, etc. Barcelona, 1734, 4to.
—— Another edition. Nuevamente corregida en esta última impression. Barcelona, 1768, 4to.
——Another edition. Trabajos de Persiles y Sigismunda, etc. 2 tom. Madrid, 1781, 8vo.
——Another edition. 2 tom. Madrid, 1799, 12mo.
——Another edition. 2 tom. Madrid, 1802, 8vo.
——Another edition. 3 vols. Madrid, 1805, 8vo.
——Nueva edicion. (Por D. M. F. de Navarrete.) Paris, 1841, 8vo.
Tom. xxvi. of the "Coleccion de los mejores Autores Españoles."
——Another edition. Madrid, 1880, 16mo.
——The Travels of Persiles and Sigismunda. Translated into French and now into English. London, 1619, 4to.
——The Wanderings of Persiles and Sigismunda. [Translated by L. D. S.—i.e., Louisa Dorothea Stanley.] London, 1854 [1853], 8vo.

IX. VIAGE DEL PARNASO.

Viage del Parnaso. Por la viuda de A. Martin : Madrid, 1614, 8vo.

——Journey to Parnassus, translated into English tercets, with preface and illustrative notes, by J. Y. Gibson. To which are subjoined the antique text and translation of the letter of Cervantes to M. Vazquez. London, 1883, 8vo.

X. EXTRACTS.

El espíritu de M. de Cervantes y Saavedra, ó la filosofia de este grande ingenio presentada en maximas, reflexiones, moralidades y agudezas sacadas de sus obras, y distribuidas por orden alfabético de materias, etc. Madrid, 1814, 8vo.
——Nueva edicion. Madrid, 1885, 12mo.
Aniversario cclx. de la Muerta de M. de Cervantes Saavedra. Album literario dedicado á la Memoria del Rey de los Ingenios Españolas. Publícalo la Redaccion de la Revista Literaria "Cervantes." Madrid, 1876, 8vo.

XI. SUPPOSITITIOUS WORKS.

Comedia de la Soberana Virgen de Guadalupe, y sus Milagros, y Grandezas de España. Sevilla, 1868, 8vo.
Published by the "Sociedad de Bibliófilos Andaluces."
The troublesome and hard adventures in love. Lively setting forth the feavers, the dangers, and the jealousies of lovers. Written in Spanish by that excellent and famous gentleman

Michael Cervantes; and exactly translated into English by R. C[ottington], Gent. London, 1652, 4to.

The diverting works of the famous Michael de Cervantes. Now first translated from the Spanish. With an introduction by the author of the London Spy [E. Ward; or rather, translated by him from the "Para todos" of J. Perez de Montalban]. London, 1709, 8vo.

A fabrication by Ward.

XII. APPENDIX.

BIOGRAPHY, CRITICISM, ETC.

Arboli, S.—Oracion fúnebre que por encargo de la Real Academia Española y en las honras de Miguel de Cervántes, etc. Madrid, 1876, 8vo.

Aruesen-Kall, B.—Den Spanske Trilogi. Studie, etc. København, 1884, 8vo.

Cervantes, pp. 12-46.

Asensio y Toledo, José Maria.— Nuevos documentos para ilustrar la vida de Miguel de Cervantes Saavedra, etc. Sevilla, 1864, 4to.

——El Conde de Lemos, protector de Cervantes. Estudio histórico, etc. Madrid, 1880, 8vo.

Baumstark, Reinhold.—Cervantes. Ein spanisches Lebensbild. Freiburg im Breisgau, 1875, 8vo.

Benavides y Navarrete, F. de P. —Oracion fúnebre que por encargo de la Real Academia Española y en las honras de Miguel de Cervantes, etc. Madrid, 1863, 8vo.

Bonterwek, Frederick.—History of Spanish and Portuguese Literature. Translated by Thomasina Ross. 2 vols. London, 1823, 8vo.

Cervantes, vol. i., pp. 327-358.

Bragge, W.—Brief Hand List of the Cervantes Collection presented to the Birmingham Free Library. [Birmingham, 1874], 8vo.

Casenave, J. M.—El Ayer y el Hoy de Miguel de Cervantes Saavedra. Valladolid, 1877, 8vo.

Cervantes, Miguel de.—Aparicion nocturna de Miguel de Cervantes á Don F. Caballero, por el Corresponsal de los Muertos. Madrid, 1841, 8vo.

——Real Academia Sevillana de Buenas Letras. Certámen Poética para commemorar el Aniversario cclvii. de la Muerte de Cervantes. Sevilla, 1873, 8vo.

——Aniversario de Cervantes. Fiesta Literaria verificada en el Instituto de Cadiz para commemorar la muerte del Principe de nuestros Ingenios. 2 pts. Cadiz, 1874-5, 8vo.

——Real Academia Sevillana de Buenas Letras. Commemoracion del Aniversario cclxi. de la Muerte de Cervantes en el dia 23 Abril de 1877. Sevilla, 1877 8vo.

——Aniversario cclxii. de la muerte de Miguel de Cervantes Saavedra. Libro compuesto para honrar la memoria del principe de los ingenios Españolas por sus admiradores de Chile. Santiago de Chile, 1878, 8vo.

Chasles, Émile. — Michel de Cervantes, sa vie, son temps, son œuvre politique et littéraire. Paris, 1866, 8vo.

Dorer, Edmund.—Cervantes und seine Werke nach deutschen Urtheilen. Mit einem Anhange: Die Cervantes Bibliographie. Leipzig, 1881, 8vo.

Entremés. — El Entremés de Refranes. ¿ Es de Cervantes? Estudio critico-literario por O. Cayetano Vidal de Valenciano. Barcelona, 1883, 8vo.

Espino, R. A. — Miscelánea Literaria. Burgos, 1886, 8vo. Un entremes de Cervántes, pp. 189-205; Otro entremes de Cervántes, pp. 207-227.

Fernandez, C.—Oracion fúnebre que por encargo de la Real Academia Española y en las honras de Miguel de Cervantes, etc. Madrid, 1867, 8vo.

Fernandez ne Navarrete, M.—Vida de Miguel de Cervantes Saavedra, escrita e ilustrada por D. M. Fernandez de Navarrete, etc. Madrid, 1819, 8vo.

Feuilleret, H. — Le Captif, ou Aventures de Michel Cervantès. Paris, 1859, 8vo.

Foronda, Manual de.—Cervantes viajero, etc. Madrid, 1880, 8vo.

Gallardo y Victor, M.—Memoria escrita sobre el rescate de Cervantes, etc. Cadiz, 1876, 8vo.

Giles, Henry. — Illustrations of Genius, etc. Boston, 1854, 8vo. Cervantes, pp. 7-29; Don Quixote, pp. 30-65.

Hagberg, Charles A.—Cervantes et Walter Scott, parallèle littéraire, etc. Lund, 1838, 8vo.

Honeywater, Ricardo Don.—The Cornutor of Seventy-five. Being a genuine narrative of the life, adventures, and amours of Don R. Honeywater. Written originally in Spanish, by the author of Don Quixote (Cervantes, or rather by John Douglas), etc. London [1748], 8vo.

——Second edition. London [1748 ?], 8vo.

Igartuburu, L. de.—Dicionario de tropos y figuras de retorica, con ejemplos de Cervantes. Madrid, 1842, 8vo.

Jimenez, F. de Paula.—Oracion funebre que por encargo de la Real Academia Española, y en las honras de Miguel de Cervantes, etc. Madrid, 1864, 8vo.

King, Alice.—A Cluster of Lives. Second edition. London, 1874, 8vo. Cervantes, pp. 215-229.

Langford, John A.—Prison Books and their authors. London, 1861, 8vo. Cervantes, pp. 58-82.

Latour, Antoine de.—Études sur l'Espagne, etc. Paris, 1855, 8vo. Cervantes à Seville, tom. i., pp. 253-291.

Louveau, E.—De Manie dans Cervantes. Thèse, etc. Montpellier, 1876, 4to.

Mainez, R. L.—Cartas literarias por el bachiller Cervantico. Cadiz, 1868, 8vo.

Mayans y Siscar, G.—Vida de Miguel de Cervantes Saavedra. Briga-Real, 1737, 8vo.

——Vida de Miguel de Cervantes Saavedra, etc. Quinta Impresion. Madrid, 1750, 8vo.

——The Life of Michael de Cervantes Saavedra. Translated by Mr. Ozell. London, 1738, 4to.

Moran, Jerónimo.—Vida de Miguel de Cervantes Saavedra. Madrid, 1863, 4to.

Muret, Th. — Michel Cervantès, drame en vers. Paris, 1856, 12mo.

Oliphant, M. O. — Cervantes. Edinburgh, 1880, 8vo.
Part of the " Foreign Classics for English Readers."

Picatoste y Rodriguez, F. — Le casa de Cervantes en Valladolid. Madrid, 1888, 8vo.

Prescott, W. H.—Biographical and Critical Essays. London, 1855, 8vo.
Cervantes, pp. 67-94.

Rementería y Fica, M.—Honores tributados á la memoria de Miguel Cervantes Saavedra en la capital de Espagne en el primer año del reinado de Isabel II., etc. Madrid, 1834, 8vo.

Roscoe, Thomas.—The Life and Writings of Miguel de Cervantes Saavedra, etc. London, 1839, 12mo.
No. 39 of the "Family Library." Compiled from Navarrete.

Segovia, A. M. — Cervantes. Nueva Utopia, monumento nacional de eterna gloria imaginado en honra del principe de los ingenios. Madrid, 1861, 8vo.

- - Ticknor, George. — History of Spanish Literature. 3 vols. Boston, 1872, 8vo.
Cervantes, vol. ii., pp. 107-179, etc.

Urdaneta, A. — Cervántes y la critica. Caracas, 1877, 8vo.

Vidart, Luis. — Cervantes, poeta épico. Apuntes críticos. Madrid, 1877, 8vo.

——Algunas ideas de Cervantes referentes á la literatura preceptiva, etc. Madrid, 1878. 8vo.

—Watts, H. E.—Cervantes. (*Encyclopædia Britannica*. Ninth edition, vol. v.) London, 1876, 4to.

MAGAZINE ARTICLES.

Cervantes, Miguel de. Semanario Pintoresco, by J. de La Revilla, 1840, pp. 329-332.—Bentley's Miscellany, vol. 24, 1848, pp. 626, 627. — Dublin University Magazine, vol. 68, 1866, pp. 123-138 ; same article, Catholic World, vol. 4, 1867, pp. 14-28. —Month, vol. 7, 1867, pp. 50-62.—Argosy, by Alice King, vol. 7, 1869, pp. 117-122.—La Ilustracion Española, by F. M. Tubino, 1872, pp. 250, 251.— All the Year Round, vol. 37, N.S., 1886, pp. 534-539.

——*and Beaumont and Fletcher.* Fraser's Magazine, vol. 91, 1875, pp. 592-597.

——*and his Writings.* American Monthly Magazine, vol. 7, 1836, pp. 342-354.

——*and Lope de Vega.* Sharpe's London Journal, by F. Lawrence, vol. 11, p. 228.

——*El Buscapié.* Dublin Review, vol. 26, 1849, pp. 137-152.

——*Caractère historique et moral du Don Quichotte.* Revue des Deux Mondes, by Émile Montégut, tom. 50, 1864, pp. 170-195.

——*Cervantes fué ó no poeta?* Semanario Pintoresco, by A. de Castro, 1851, pp. 354, 355.

——*La Cocina del Quijote.* La Ilustracion Español, 1872, pp. 533-539, 554, 555, 566-570.

Cervantes, Miguel de.

——Comentarios filosóficos del Quijote. Cronica Hispano-Americana, by N. D. Benjumea, 1859, Nos. 14, 15, 16, 17, 18, 19, 20.

——Congeturas sobre el funda-mento que pudo tener la idea que dió origen á la patraña de el Buscapié. Revista de Ciencias, Literatura y Artes, by C. A. de la Barrera, tom. 2, 1856, pp. 731-741.

——Découverte du véritable por-trait de Cervantes. Revue Bri-tannique, by A. de Latour, 9 Série, 1865, pp. 471-485.

——Don Quixote. Blackwood's Edinburgh Magazine, vol. 11, 1822, pp. 657-668. — North American Review, by W. H. Prescott, vol. 45, 1837, pp. 1-34.—Revue Française, by A. Nisard, vol. 7, 1838, pp. 299-327. — Knickerbocker, by R. J. de Cordova, vol. 38, 1851, pp. 189-203.—Westminster Re-view, vol. 33, N.S., 1868, pp. 299-327; same article, Eclectic Magazine, vol. 8, N.S., pp. 909-925.—Cornhill Magazine, vol. 30, 1874, pp. 595-616.

—— ——and Gil Blas. Penn Monthly, by C. H. Drew, vol. 3, 1872, pp. 555-564.

—— ——Duffield's Translation. Blackwood's Edinburgh Maga-zine, vol. 130, 1881, pp. 469-490.

—— ——Episodes of Don Quixote. London Magazine, vol. 6, N.S., 1826, pp. 557-566 ; vol. 7, N.S., 1827, pp. 11-19.

—— ——Heine on Don Quixote. Temple Bar, vol. 48, 1876, pp. 235-249.

Cervantes, Miguel de.

—— ——Jarvis's Translation of Don Quixote. Monthly Review, vol. 3, N.S., 1837, pp. 230-240.

—— ——Library of Don Quixote. Fraser's Magazine, vol. 7, 1833, pp. 324-331, 565-577.

—— ——Ormsby's Translation of Don Quixote. Quarterly Re-view, vol. 162, 1886, pp. 43-79.

—Saturday Review, June 13, 1885, pp. 794, 795.—Nation, vol. 41, 1885, pp. 513, 514, 535-537.

—— ——Rambles in the Footsteps of Don Quixote. Dublin Uni-versity Magazine, vol. 11, 1838, pp. 574-581.

——Drama of. Gentleman's Magazine, by J. Mew, vol. 23, N.S., 1879, pp. 446-470.

——Educacion cientifica de Cer-vantes. El Museo Universal, by N. D. Benjumea, tom. 13, 1869, pp. 19-22, 38, 39.

——Entremeses. Gentleman's Magazine, by James Mew, 1881, pp. 451-469.

——Estatua de Cervantes. Sema-nario Pintoresco, 1836, pp. 249-253.

——Galatea. Gentleman's Maga-zine, by James Mew, 1880, pp. 670-690.

——Life of. United States Liter-ary Gazette, vol. 2, 1827, pp. 415-427.—Monthly Review, vol. 2, N.S., 1834, pp. 383-395.—North American Review, by E. Wigglesworth, vol. 38, 1834, pp. 277-307.—North American Review, by W. H. Prescott, vol. 45, 1837, pp. 1-34.

——Nota de las Personas que intervienen en la Historia del Ingeniosa Hidalgo Don Quijote.

Cervantes, Miguel de.
Semanario Pintoresco, by R. Salomon, 1850, pp. 129-134.
——*Notas á la Vida de Cervantes.* Revista de Ciencias, Literatura y Artes, by C. A. de la Barrera, tom. 3, 1856, pp. 468-478.
——*Novels.* Gentleman's Magazine, by James Mew, 1878, pp. 358-372; 1879, pp. 95-110.
——*Observaciones sobre las Ediciones primitivas del Ingenioso Hidalgo Don Quijote de la Mancha.* Revista de España, by José Maria Asensio, tom. 9, 1869, pp. 367-376.
——*Un Paseo á la Patria de Don Quijote.* Semanario Pintoresco, by J. Jimenez-Serrano, 1848, pp. 19-22, 35-37, 41-43, 109-111, 131-133.
——*Le Portrait de Cervantes.* Revue Germanique, by J. M.

Cervantes, Miguel de.
Guardia, tom. 38, 1866, pp. 300-314.
——*Recuerdos de Cervantes.* Semanario Pintoresco, by J. Jiminez-Serrano, 1848, pp. 161-163.
——*Resumen por orden cronologico, de las principales aventuras del Ingenioso Hidalgo Don Quijote.* Semanario Pintoresco, by R. Salomon, 1850, pp. 148-151.
——*Significacion histórica de Cervantes.* Cronica Hispano-Americana, by N. Benjumea, tom. 3, 1859, pp. 8, 9.
——*La Tia Fingida.* El Criticon, by B. J. Gallardo, No. 1, 1835.
——*Viage de Cervantes á Italia.* El Museo Universal, by N. D. Benjumea, tom. 13, 1869, pp. 102, 103, 110.
——*Voyage to Parnassus.* Gentleman's Magazine, by James Mew, 1880, pp. 81-93.

XIII. CHRONOLOGICAL LIST OF WORKS.

THE WALTER SCOTT PRESS, NEWCASTLE-ON-TYNE.

NEW BOOKS

IMPORTED BY

CHARLES SCRIBNER'S SONS,

NEW YORK CITY.

Crown 8vo, Cloth. Price 1.25 per Volume.

THE

CONTEMPORARY SCIENCE SERIES.

EDITED BY HAVELOCK ELLIS.

Illustrated Volumes, containing between 300 and 400 pp.

THE CONTEMPORARY SCIENCE SERIES is bringing within general reach of the English-speaking public the best that is known and thought in all departments of modern scientific research. The influence of the scientific spirit is now rapidly spreading in every field of human activity. Social progress, it is felt, must be guided and accompanied by accurate knowledge,—knowledge which is, in many departments, not yet open to the English reader. In the Contemporary Science Series all the questions of modern life—the various social and politico-economical problems of to-day, the most recent researches in the knowledge of man, the past and present experiences of the race, and the nature of its environment—are frankly investigated and clearly presented.

Already Published:—

THE EVOLUTION OF SEX. By Prof. PATRICK GEDDES and J. ARTHUR THOMSON. 90 Illustrations, and 322 pages.

" A work which, for range and grace, mastery of material, originality, and incisiveness of style and treatment, is not readily to be matched in the long list of books designed more or less to popularise science. . . . The series will be, if it goes on as it has begun, one of the most valuable now current."—*Scottish Leader.*

" The book is the opening volume of a new Scientific Series, and the publishers are to be congratulated on starting with such a model of scientific exposition."—*Scotsman.*

New York: CHARLES SCRIBNER'S SONS.

ELECTRICITY IN MODERN LIFE. By G. W. DE
TUNZELMANN. With 88 Illustrations, and 272 pages.

" It is with much pleasure that we call attention to this volume, for the
author has very successfully grappled with the difficulty of placing so intricate
a subject in a form simple and plain enough to be understood by the ordinary
reader. . . . The volume is illustrated by numerous carefully-drawn pictures
and diagrams."—*Guardian.*

THE ORIGIN OF THE ARYANS. By Dr. ISAAC TAYLOR.
With 30 Illustrations, and 339 pages.

" Canon Taylor is probably the most encyclopædic all-round scholar now
living. For wide range of knowledge and depth of reading he could no doubt
give points even to Mr. Herbert Spencer. . . . His new volume on the Origin
of the Aryans is a first-rate example of the excellent account to which he can
turn his exceptionally wide and varied information. . . . Masterly and
exhaustive."—*Pall Mall Gazette.*

PHYSIOGNOMY AND EXPRESSION. (Illustrated.) By
P. MANTEGAZZA. 336 pages.

" A good, popular treatment of the subject of physiognomy, which should
embody the results of recent scientific inquiry, was decidedly a desideratum,
and in the volume before us we have the want very adequately met."—
Sheffield Independent.

EVOLUTION AND DISEASE. By J. BLAND SUTTON, F.R.C.S.
With 137 Illustrations, and 304 pages.

" The publisher and editor of the series, and the ingenious author certainly
deserve congratulation, for the book opens up from a distance what seemed a
very dark country, and proves that many diseases are neither unnatural nor
unintelligible, and that pathology is not necessarily pessimistic."—*Scottish
Leader.*

THE VILLAGE COMMUNITY. With special reference to its
Survivals in Britain. By G. LAURENCE GOMME, Director of the
Folk-Lore Society. With Numerous Maps and Plans.

" Mr. Gomme, while considering generally the Aryan local institutions as
developed in Europe and Asia, has devoted special attention to Village
Communities in England. He has gone to the best sources, and has told us
practically all that we can at present know about the way in which village life
has been organised and developed."—*London Echo.*

THE CRIMINAL. By HAVELOCK ELLIS. With many Illus-
trations.

" As a clever summary of all there is at present to say upon a socially most
important question, the book should widely be welcomed."—*Yorkshire Post.*

" The author's own views concerning the lines of reform are expressed with
candour, moderation, and an utter absence of extravagance ; but they are of
less importance than the vast body of fact which he has brought together with
such industry and enthusiasm. The book may be described as a pioneer
volume, and as such it cannot fail to be useful."—*Manchester Examiner.*

SANITY AND INSANITY. By Dr. C. MERCIER.

"Taken as a whole, it is the brightest book on the physical side of mental science published in our time."—*Pall Mall Gazette.*

"A more ably written and vigorously thought book on the subject of which it treats it would be difficult to find."—*Scottish Leader.*

HYPNOTISM. By Dr. ALBERT MOLL (Berlin).

"Of all the works published on the subject, from that of La Fontaine, the French Magnetiser, who made public experiments in Manchester in 1841, down to the records of the modern school at Nancy, Dr. Moll's work is the one most likely to appeal to the ordinary lay reader."—*Galignani's Messenger.*

MANUAL TRAINING. By Dr. C. M. WOODWARD, Director of the Manual Training School, Washington University, St. Louis, Mo. Illustrated.

"There is no greater authority on the subject of manual training than Professor Woodward. . . . Professor Woodward is not less instructive as a practical man than as a theorist, and his book may be confidently recommended to those who wish to know what may be done and what has been done in America in the direction of systematic instruction of this kind."—*Manchester Guardian.*

THE SCIENCE OF FAIRY TALES. By E. S. HARTLAND.

"Mr. Hartland's book will win the sympathy of all earnest students, both by the knowledge it displays, and by a thorough love and appreciation of his subject, which is evident throughout."—*The Spectator.*

PRIMITIVE FOLK. Studies in Comparative Ethnology. By ELIE RECLUS.

"A more suggestive book, with less of pedantry, could not be imagined."—*Birmingham Daily Gazette.*

BACTERIA AND THEIR PRODUCTS. By Dr. SIMS WOODHEAD.

"A singularly able and informative exposition of the present state of knowledge in regard to one of the youngest, but most practically important, departments of natural science."—*Scottish Leader.*

THE EVOLUTION OF MARRIAGE. By LETOURNEAU.

An ethnographical summary of the facts regarding the origin and growth of marriage and the family among savages, barbarians, and in civilisation, with hints as to its probable evolution in the future.

EDUCATION AND HEREDITY. By J. M. GUYAU.

A sociological study of the various modifications in education which are involved by modern scientific conceptions and modern conditions of civilisation. It deals with the influence of education in the development of the race, with the effects of heredity in education, with the place of physical education, and with the objects and methods of education generally.

New York : CHARLES SCRIBNER'S SONS.

THE MAN OF GENIUS. By Prof. LOMBROSO.

This work is a translation of Prof. Lombroso's *L'Uomo di Genio* (the largest and most important work yet written on Genius), made with the co-operation of another authority, who has supplied additional material for the English edition. The work deals with the causes of genius; the influences of race, of heredity, of climate, of great cities; the mental and physical characteristics of men of genius in literature, art, politics, and religion; and goes fully into the much-debated question of the relation between genius and insanity. The volume will be copiously illustrated.

PUBLIC HEALTH. By Dr. J. F. J. SYKES.

THE SPIRIT OF SCIENCE. By Prof. KARL PEARSON.

Other volumes to follow at short intervals, including "The Laws of Life in Language," "The Development of Electro-Magnetic Theory," "Industrial Development," "The Factors of Evolution," "Wages," etc., etc.

The following Writers are preparing volumes for this Series:—
Prof. E. D. Cope, Prof. G. F. Fitzgerald, Prof. J. Geikie, E. C. K. Gonner, Prof. J. Jastrow (Wisconsin), Prof. C. H. Herford, Prof. Haddon, etc., etc.

IBSEN'S FAMOUS PROSE DRAMAS.

(COMPLETE IN FIVE VOLUMES.)

EDITED BY WILLIAM ARCHER.

12mo, *CLOTH, PRICE* $1.25 *PER VOLUME.*

VOL. I.

With Portrait of the Author, and Biographical Introduction by WILLIAM ARCHER.

This volume contains—"A DOLL'S HOUSE," "THE LEAGUE OF YOUTH" (*never before translated*), and "THE PILLARS OF SOCIETY."

VOL. II.

"GHOSTS," "AN ENEMY OF THE PEOPLE," and "THE WILD DUCK." With an Introductory Note by WILLIAM ARCHER.

VOL. III.

"LADY INGER OF ÖSTRÅT," "THE VIKINGS AT HELGELAND," "THE PRETENDERS." With an Introductory Note by WILLIAM ARCHER, and Portrait of Ibsen.

New York: CHARLES SCRIBNER'S SONS.

VOL. IV.
"EMPEROR AND GALILEAN." Translated by WILLIAM
ARCHER.
VOL. V.
"ROSMERSHOLM," "THE LADY FROM THE SEA,"
"HEDDA GABLER."

The sequence of the plays *in each volume* will be chronological ;
and the set of volumes comprising the dramas will thus present them,
when completed, in chronological order.

" The art of prose translation does not perhaps enjoy a very high literary
status in England, but we have no hesitation in numbering the present version
of Ibsen, so far as it has gone (Vols. I. and II.), among the very best achievements, in that kind, of our generation."—*Academy.*

GREAT WRITERS.
A NEW SERIES OF CRITICAL BIOGRAPHIES OF FAMOUS
WRITERS OF EUROPE AND AMERICA.
LIBRARY EDITION.
*Printed on large paper of extra quality, in handsome binding,
Demy 8vo, price $1.00 each.*

ALPHABETICAL LIST.
PRESS NOTICES.
Life of Jane Austen. By Goldwin Smith.
  " Mr. Goldwin Smith has added another to the not inconsiderable roll
of eminent men who have found their delight in Jane Austen. Certainly
a fascinating book."—*Spectator.*
Life of Balzac. By Frederick Wedmore.
  " A finished study, a concentrated summary, a succinct analysis of
Balzac's successes and failures, and the causes of these successes and
failures, and of the scope of his genius."—*Scottish Leader.*
Life of Charlotte Brontë. By A. Birrell.
  " Those who know much of Charlotte Brontë will learn more, and those
who know nothing about her will find all that is best worth learning in
Mr. Birrell's pleasant book."—*St. James' Gazette.*
Life of Browning. By William Sharp.
  " This little volume is a model of excellent English, and in every respect
it seems to us what a biography should be."—*Public Opinion.*

Life of Byron. By Hon. Roden Noel.

"He (Mr. Noel) has at any rate given to the world the most credible and comprehensible portrait of the poet ever drawn with pen and ink."—*Manchester Examiner.*

Life of Bunyan. By Canon Venables.

"A most intelligent, appreciative, and valuable memoir."—*Scotsman.*

Life of Burns. By Professor Blackie.

"The editor certainly made a hit when he persuaded Blackie to write about Burns."—*Pall Mall Gazette.*

Life of Thomas Carlyle. By R. Garnett, LL.D.

"This is an admirable book. Nothing could be more felicitous and fairer than the way in which he takes us through Carlyle's life and works."—*Pall Mall Gazette.*

Life of Coleridge. By Hall Caine.

"Brief and vigorous, written throughout with spirit and great literary skill."—*Scotsman.*

Life of Congreve. By Edmund Gosse.

"Mr. Gosse has written an admirable and most interesting biography of a man of letters who is of particular interest to other men of letters."—*The Academy.*

Life of Crabbe. By T. E. Kebbel.

"No English poet since Shakespeare has observed certain aspects of nature and of human life more closely; and in the qualities of manliness and of sincerity he is surpassed by none. . . . Mr. Kebbel's monograph is worthy of the subject."—*Athenæum.*

Life of Darwin. By G. T. Bettany.

"Mr. G. T. Bettany's *Life of Darwin* is a sound and conscientious work."—*Saturday Review.*

Life of Dickens. By Frank T. Marzials.

"Notwithstanding the mass of matter that has been printed relating to Dickens and his works . . . we should, until we came across this volume, have been at a loss to recommend any popular life of England's most popular novelist as being really satisfactory. The difficulty is removed by Mr. Marzials's little book."—*Athenæum.*

Life of George Eliot. By Oscar Browning.

"We are thankful for this interesting addition to our knowledge of the great novelist."—*Literary World.*

Life of Emerson. By Richard Garnett, LL.D.

"As to the larger section of the public, to whom the series of Great Writers is addressed, no record of Emerson's life and work could be more desirable, both in breadth of treatment and lucidity of style, than Dr. Garnett's."—*Saturday Review.*

Life of Goethe. By James Sime.

"Mr. James Sime's competence as a biographer of Goethe, both in respect of knowledge of his special subject, and of German literature generally, is beyond question."—*Manchester Guardian.*

Life of Goldsmith. By Austin Dobson.

"The story of his literary and social life in London, with all its humorous and pathetic vicissitudes, is here retold, as none could tell it better."—*Daily News.*

New York: CHARLES SCRIBNER'S SONS.

Life of Nathaniel Hawthorne. By Moncure Conway.
" Easy and conversational as the tone is throughout, no important fact is omitted, no useless fact is recalled."—*Speaker.*

Life of Heine. By William Sharp.
"This is an admirable monograph . . . more fully written up to the level of recent knowledge and criticism of its theme than any other English work."—*Scotsman.*

Life of Victor Hugo. By Frank T. Marzials.
" Mr. Marzials's volume presents to us, in a more handy form than any English, or even French handbook gives, the summary of what, up to the moment in which we write, is known or conjectured about the life of the great poet."—*Saturday Review.*

Life of Samuel Johnson. By Colonel F. Grant.
" Colonel Grant has performed his task with diligence, sound judgment, good taste, and accuracy."—*Illustrated London News.*

Life of Keats. By W. M. Rossetti.
"Valuable for the ample information which it contains."—*Cambridge Independent.*

Life of Lessing. By T. W. Rolleston.
" A picture of Lessing which is vivid and truthful, and has enough of detail for all ordinary purposes."—*Nation* (New York).

Life of Longfellow. By Prof. Eric S. Robertson.
" A most readable little book."—*Liverpool Mercury.*

Life of Marryat. By David Hannay.
"What Mr. Hannay had to do—give a craftsman-like account of a great craftsman who has been almost incomprehensibly undervalued—could hardly have been done better than in this little volume."—*Manchester Guardian.*

Life of Mill. By W. L. Courtney.
" A most sympathetic and discriminating memoir."—*Glasgow Herald.*

Life of Milton. By Richard Garnett, LL.D.
" Within equal compass the life-story of the great poet of Puritanism has never been more charmingly or adequately told."—*Scottish Leader.*

Life of Dante Gabriel Rossetti. By J. Knight.
" Mr. Knight's picture of the great poet and painter is the fullest and best yet presented to the public."—*The Graphic.*

Life of Scott. By Professor Yonge.
" For readers and lovers of the poems and novels of Sir Walter Scott, this is a most enjoyable book."—*Aberdeen Free Press.*

Life of Arthur Schopenhauer. By William Wallace.
" The series of 'Great Writers' has hardly had a contribution of more marked and peculiar excellence than the book which the Whyte Professor of Moral Philosophy at Oxford has written for it on the attractive and still (in England) little known subject of Schopenhauer."—*Manchester Guardian.*

Life of Shelley. By William Sharp.
" The criticisms . . . entitle this capital monograph to be ranked with the best biographies of Shelley."—*Westminster Review.*

New York: CHARLES SCRIBNER'S SONS.

Life of Sheridan. By Lloyd Sanders.

"To say that Mr. Lloyd Sanders, in this volume, has produced the best existing memoir of Sheridan is really to award much fainter praise than the book deserves."—*Manchester Examiner.*

"Rapid and workmanlike in style ; the author has evidently a good practical knowledge of the stage of Sheridan's day."—*Saturday Review.*

Life of Adam Smith. By R. B. Haldane, M.P.

"Written with a perspicuity seldom exemplified when dealing with economic science."—*Scotsman.*

"Mr. Haldane's handling of his subject impresses us as that of a man who well understands his theme, and who knows how to elucidate it."—*Scottish Leader.*

"A beginner in political economy might easily do worse than take Mr. Haldane's book as his first text-book."—*Graphic.*

Life of Smollett. By David Hannay.

"A capital record of a writer who still remains one of the great masters of the English novel."—*Saturday Review.*

"Mr. Hannay is excellently equipped for writing the life of Smollett. As a specialist on the history of the eighteenth century navy, he is at a great advantage in handling works so full of the sea and sailors as Smollett's three principal novels. Moreover, he has a complete acquaintance with the Spanish romancers, from whom Smollett drew so much of his inspiration. His criticism is generally acute and discriminating ; and his narrative is well arranged, compact, and accurate."—*St. James's Gazette.*

Life of Schiller. By Henry W. Nevinson.

"This is a well-written little volume, which presents the leading facts of the poet's life in a neatly-rounded picture."—*Scotsman.*

"Mr. Nevinson has added much to the charm of his book by his spirited translations, which give excellently both the ring and sense of the original."—*Manchester Guardian.*

Life of Thackeray. By Herman Merivale and Frank T. Marzials.

"The book, with its excellent bibliography, is one which neither the student nor the general reader can well afford to miss."—*Pall Mall Gazette.*

"The last book published by Messrs. Merivale and Marzials is full of very real and true things."—Mrs. Anne Thackeray Ritchie on "Thackeray and his Biographers," in *Illustrated London News.*

Life of Cervantes. By H. E. Watts.

Complete Bibliography to each volume, by J. P. ANDERSON, British Museum, London.

Volumes are in preparation by W. E. HENLEY, H. E. WATTS, COSMO MONKHOUSE, FRANK T. MARZIALS, W. H. POLLOCK, STEPNIAK, etc., etc.

New York : CHARLES SCRIBNER'S SONS.